LADY DIANA'S DARING DEED

Mona Gedney

ZEBRA BOOKS
Kensington Publishing Corp.
http://www.zebrabooks.com

12709408

ZEBRA BOOKS are published by

Kensington Publishing Corp.
850 Third Avenue
New York, NY 10022

All Kensington titles, imprints and distributed lines are available at special quantity discounts for bulk purchases for sales promotion, premiums, fund raising, educational or institutional use.

Special book excerpts or customized printings can also be created to fit specific needs. For details, write or phone the office of the Kensington Special Sales Manager: Kensington Publishing Corp., 850 Third Avenue, New York, NY, 10022, Attn. Special Sales Department. Phone: 1-800-221-2647.

First Printing: November, 2000
10 9 8 7 6 5 4 3 2 1

Printed in the United States of America

FIRST KISS

"I wrote an announcement yesterday," Diana replied, "for I have always found that unpleasant duties should be faced at once."

"And did you send it?" he demanded, moving closer and attempting to look her in the eye.

Diana continued to smooth the wrinkle on her skirt until he cupped his hand under her chin and forced her to look up at him. "Would that be so very terrible, Mr. Melville?" she inquired gently, forcing herself not to react to his unexpected movement. "After all, we are engaged, are we not?"

"You forget, ma'am, that I must ask your uncle's permission before taking such a public step," he replied smoothly.

Her first reaction to his hand under her chin had been to strike it away, but two things stopped her— the memory of what she was trying to accomplish— and the arresting depth of his green eyes.

"And you forget yourself, sir, to make so free with me," Diana responded, still looking into his eyes. "Perhaps you mistake me for one of your flirts."

"Not at all," said Melville, putting his free arm around her waist and pulling her from her chair. "Those ladies do not make the mistake of attempting to rule me," he murmured, kissing her soundly. . . .

Books by Mona Gedney

A LADY OF FORTUNE

THE EASTER CHARADE

A VALENTINE'S DAY GAMBIT

A CHRISTMAS BETROTHAL

A SCANDALOUS CHARADE

A DANGEROUS AFFAIR

A LADY OF QUALITY

A DANGEROUS ARRANGEMENT

MERRY'S CHRISTMAS

LADY DIANA'S DARING DEED

Published by Zebra Books

One

Lady Diana Ballinger stared from her carriage window at the noisy, bustling streets and smiled. It had been over a year since her last visit to London and she had waited impatiently for her twin brother Trevor to leave Cambridge and come to town to live so that she and their aunt could join him.

"It's wonderful to be back again, isn't it, Aunt Lavinia?" she sighed contentedly, leaning back against the leather seat. "We've been waiting for ages! Haven't you missed all of this?"

"Of course I have," replied her aunt affectionately, reaching over to smooth Diana's dark curls, which had been ruffled by the spring breeze that swept through the open carriage windows. "Perhaps not as much as you have, though. I don't require as much excitement as you and Trevor."

"What shall we do first?" demanded Diana eagerly. "Should we go shopping or to Gunter's for an ice?" Seeing her aunt's doubtful expression, she added enticingly, "Or perhaps we should go to Hookham's. I know that you've finished the last of the Gothic novels you got at Leamington, and you could pick up some new ones."

Lavinia Ballinger was a small, plump woman, comfortable and cheerful, but just then even this appeal to her greatest weakness failed, and a small frown creased her usually smooth brow. She gave the ribbons of her bonnet an anxious tug, unconsciously pulling it rather rakishly over one ear as she settled back against the leather squabs.

"I'm afraid, Diana, that the first thing we should do is to write to your Uncle Robert. He is going to be amazingly cross when he hears that we have actually arrived in London and taken a house. I've been thinking about that all during our journey. You know that he will say that we should have waited to write to him for permission even to come to town, and here we are, setting up for the rest of the Season."

"Oh, bother Uncle Robert!" replied Diana crossly, her expression darkening. "He would stop us from having the least bit of pleasure if he could! We can write to him later and he can preach to us just as well then."

"Never fear. He will do precisely that," returned her aunt, resigning herself to her fate. She had never been a match for the combined wills of her niece and nephew, and so she had decided to conserve her strength rather than work against them. "He will certainly call me to account, which I'm accustomed to, of course, but I'm afraid that you will also have to answer to him—and perhaps Trevor will, too, since he has made the arrangements for our house. It is such a shame that we aren't taking the house for a longer time so that the dear boy could move in with us, but there's no point in his moving in only to have to turn around and move back in with Tom again."

As they neared North Audley Street, the location of the house she and her niece were to share, Lavinia straightened up as well as her partridge-plump figure would allow and firmly set her hat to rights. She had never been one to cry over spilt milk.

"Since we know what is to come when your uncle discovers what we've done," she observed cheerfully, "I suppose that we had best set about enjoying ourselves immediately. We will deal with your uncle when the time comes."

"You are the best of aunts!" exclaimed Diana, hugging her and once again setting her hat awry. "We won't let you face Uncle Robert alone!"

Diana had every intention of following her aunt's advice. Experience had taught her to make the most of every moment. One could never be certain when Uncle Robert would arrive on the scene and put an end to pleasure.

Orphaned when they were eight, she and Trevor had been left to the none-too-tender mercies of their elderly bachelor uncle. Robert Barton was a wealthy man himself, and he had strongly disapproved of his sister's marriage, even though she had captured an earl. He had thought the former earl, who had been a cheerful, sociable man, quite a "loose screw," and he hadn't thought that his sister should have been exposed either to "the evils of such a man" or to those of the society into which he had taken her—and into which she had happily gone.

Fortunately for the twins, his powers over them were limited in many respects. Their father had had great faith in his brother-in-law's integrity and his financial astuteness but none at all in his disposition, so he had provided very specifically for his children's emotional well-being. The schools that Trevor was to attend had been specified in the will, and both twins had been guaranteed the society of both Lady Lavinia Ballinger, their father's maiden sister, and a governess and tutor chosen by that lady.

Otherwise, the pair would have found themselves in most unhappy circumstances, living in the far north of England with a man whose disposition and home closely resembled the bleak winters of that country. Since both of them had their parents' happy, easygoing nature, such a fate would have been bitter indeed. With Lady Lavinia, their lives had been cheerful and busy, darkened only by brief visits to Northumberland and by their uncle's periodic stays with them, during which he complained unceasingly of their levity and of Lady Lavinia's lack of control over them.

Unfortunately, although their aunt was the one to live with them, it was their uncle who was in charge of their fortunes. Since Trevor frequently found himself overextended, this had periodically presented a problem. However, as long as Trevor was in school, he had rubbed along reasonably well with the periodic donation of Diana's pin money and their aunt's small contributions; though since she was a lady of limited circumstances, they had tried to avoid overtaxing her slender resources. The will provided generously for her home and carriage and all the necessities of her life, but her brother had not thought to increase the amount of the quarterly allowance that he gave her while he was alive, not realizing that he regularly gave her far more than that as gifts. It was an oversight that Trevor had sworn to remedy when he came of age.

Their father had left his children a generous annual allowance for travel and wardrobe, and it was from that fund that they had managed to take a house in town for the spring months. All three of them—Lavinia, Trevor, and Diana—were fully aware that Diana should have applied to Robert Barton for permission to leave the country home near Leamington Spa where she lived with Lavinia. They were also fully aware that he might very well have withheld that permission because of his distaste for life in London; he frequently commented that his sister's death had come all too soon after her removal to that "den of iniquity." Diana also had no doubt that he did not believe that exposure to London would improve what he considered her careless, light-minded behavior.

Trevor, as he finished his course of studies and approached his twenty-first birthday, had at least enjoyed a little more freedom of movement than his sister, whose restricted situation had sorely tried her patience. No matter how severe the scolding from her uncle, Diana reflected that even a fortnight in London was worth the price. If all went well, she would have several months.

"Look, Aunt! There he is!"

Her aunt, still thinking of the scolding, clutched her throat. "Mr. Barton is here, Diana? Where? However did he discover us so quickly?"

"No, you goose!" laughed her unrepentant niece. "Not Uncle Robert—Trevor!"

And, despite Lavinia's protests at her lack of propriety, Diana poked her head out the window and waved wildly to her brother, who was strolling along the sidewalk with another gentleman.

"Trevor!" she called, attracting the interest of a number of other passers-by as the carriage rolled to a stop. A silent Diana would have attracted attention simply because of her striking appearance—dark, curling hair against creamy skin and sparkling eyes that seemed almost black—but an animated Diana, waving and smiling, was enough to stop traffic.

"By all that's wonderful, Di! I hadn't expected you until tomorrow! Welcome to your new home!" Opening the door before the footman could do so, the Earl of Landford swept a low bow and started to extend his hand, but his sister had already hopped nimbly down and thrown her arms around his neck, ignoring her aunt's audible moan at this new indiscretion.

"It's been ages since Christmas, Trevor! How wonderful to see you again—and to see you here!"

Turning to his blushing friend who was watching this onslaught with silent admiration, Trevor grinned. "So what do you think, Tom? Has she changed since you saw her last?"

Young Lord Ralston shook his head, stammering. "Not an iota. You—you look grand, Lady Diana. As do you, Lady Lavinia," he added hurriedly, mindful of his manners.

Diana shook his hand warmly. "And when did I become 'Lady Diana,' Tom?" she teased. "Don't you remember chasing me around the garden playing blindman's buff? I was just Diana then."

"But we were only children then, Di!" protested Lord Ralston, turning scarlet and temporarily reverting to childhood. "Barely out of leading strings! Now you're a young lady!"

"Do keep telling her that, Tom," sighed her aunt, as Trevor helped her from the carriage and hugged her. "I haven't been able to convince her of it, try as I may."

"Stuff and nonsense!" exclaimed Diana, her smile and light tone taking away the sharpness of her words. "You know that there's no hope of it, Aunt!"

"Truer words were never spoken, ma'am," agreed Trevor in an unnaturally deep voice, "and, as the head of this family, I feel that I must insist upon your behaving in a manner that will make you a credit to the family. In fact, I must insist that—"

"Enough!" protested Diana, laughing and holding up her hands in mock surrender. "I'll swear that you sound more like Uncle Robert every time you do that, Trev."

Her brother's eyes widened dramatically and he shook his head decidedly, thinning his lips into a straight, unsmiling line. "I must give it up immediately if this is your reaction," he said sternly, maintaining his deep voice, "for laughing too much is characteristic of an indifferent intelligence and I, for one, do not intend to be a party to leading one of my own flesh and blood astray by being the cause of such behavior."

Here he eyed his sister sternly and shook his head. "And I see, Missy," he continued, using the name their uncle had given her in childhood, the one that still caused her skin to crawl, "that you are far too easily led. That is why we must keep you away from that den of iniquity that calls itself the capital of this fair land! Get thee to a nunnery, my girl!"

"I go immediately, sir," she responded modestly, curtseying with her eyes downcast. "I shall renounce the world and take my vows of poverty, chastity, and obedience."

"For heaven's sake, Trevor, take her in off the streets and out of the public eye before she says something else outrageous," moaned their horrified aunt, trying to ignore several admiring gentlemen who had turned to smile at them. "There's no telling what the two of you will do next."

Once Trevor had taken them on a tour of their house and had the footman carry their luggage to their rooms, he waited impatiently for them to join him in the drawing room.

"What is it that's so urgent that you can't wait to tell us, Trev?" demanded his sister as she settled beside him on the sofa.

"Yes, Trevor, what is it?" echoed Aunt Lavinia. "I'm still coated with the dust of the road, so I trust that all this rush is needful."

Trevor took her hands and lowered her to the sofa on the other side of him. "It is, Aunt Lavinia. I swear that it is!" he assured her, his startlingly dark eyes, precisely like those of his sister, fixed upon her.

"Well, then," she said more warmly, "I can see by your expression that it is indeed important. Do tell us what it is, dear boy."

"Yes, Trevor, don't keep us in suspense. You know

that's what you like to do—just as you did at Christmas when you made us wait for days before you told us that you were going to take this house for us in the spring."

"What I'm going to tell you is much more important than that," he assured her. "This is—well, it's something that will change my whole life!" Pleased with his statement, he sank back against the velvet cushions of the sofa in satisfaction.

Both ladies regarded him with astonishment, but for the moment he appeared to have done with speaking. His dreamy gaze told them clearly that he was miles away from them.

"What is it, Trev? Do stop daydreaming and explain!" demanded Diana, shaking his arm. "Are you purchasing a pair of colors? Have you decided to join the Guard? What are you talking about?"

For a few moments he didn't answer, and Lavinia shook her head at Diana. "No, indeed, my dear. Trevor is in love."

At her words, he seemed suddenly to come to life and beamed at her. "Oh, yes, Aunt Lavinia! How wise you are to recognize it!"

"In love?" repeated Diana blankly. "With whom? Is it another opera singer that you've met?" Trevor had visited London in the fall and had promptly fallen under the spell of a knowledgeable young lady known to her and her aunt only as Miss Nell.

"Of course not!" he returned indignantly. "That was merely an infatuation—and fortunately it was over with before Uncle Robert ever heard of it. *This* is not an infatuation—it is a lifelong devotion."

"But how could you be in love, Trevor?" Diana

asked again, returning to her theme. "You never said a word about any such thing in your letters."

"That's because I wanted you to meet her—not just to read about her in my pitiful little notes. I could never do Jenny justice in a letter."

"Jenny?" repeated Diana encouragingly, glad to have at least one specific detail. "Jenny who, Trevor? Tell us about her."

"Yes, my dear, do tell us about your young lady," agreed Aunt Lavinia, patting his hand.

"She's unbelievably lovely, Aunt," he replied, turning to her eagerly, "lovelier than any princess in the fairy tales you used to read to us. Her eyes are the color of cornflowers and her hair is like spun gold. And she is kind. I've never known a woman to have so tender and loving a heart."

"Trevor!" Diana shook his arm, trying to get his attention. She had never heard her brother speak like this about any of his other ladyloves. "Just who is Jenny and when did you meet her?"

"Jenny Linden," he sighed dreamily. "Lady Genevieve, that is."

Lavinia stirred uneasily. "You don't mean Lord Appelby's child, do you, Trevor? I knew him years ago when I was a girl."

He seized her hands and pressed them ecstatically. "Yes, Aunt. Jenny is Lord Appelby's eldest daughter."

"And Appelby," his aunt asked carefully, "what does he think of your suit?"

"Oh, I haven't said anything to him yet, Aunt, but I will—very soon. In fact, I was just waiting to tell you two before I approached him."

"And Jenny," said Diana, smiling at her brother's eagerness, "is she as smitten as you are?"

"Will you think me cork-brained—or lacking in gallantry—if I say she is?" he responded, smiling back at her.

"I would think her very sensible," returned Diana firmly. "How could she fail to love you?"

"But Trevor," said his aunt slowly, "what of your uncle? Should you not speak with him before taking such a step?"

Both of them stared at her a moment, the unpleasant truth of what she had said settling over them like a damp woolen blanket.

"He couldn't be so cruel as to refuse you permission!" cried Diana.

"You know that he could do just that, Di," said Trevor, rubbing his hands through his dark hair until it stood up in spikes. "It's exactly the kind of thing that would give him pleasure."

"Well, if by some miracle he were to approve the match, you would come into your fortune now instead of when you're twenty-five," mused Aunt Lavinia, patting his hair back into place. "Perhaps he would be glad to see you settled, Trevor. It may well be that he would think marriage would have a calming effect upon you."

"Not Uncle Robert!" returned Trevor hotly, rising from the sofa and striding up and down the room. "If he saw that he could spoke my wheel, he would do so in an instant! I'm certain that he would tell me to wait until I am twenty-five, assuring me that it would be good for me."

"That would be quite a long engagement," observed Diana dubiously. "Surely he wouldn't think that wise."

"It wouldn't matter to him! When has he ever thought of our happiness?"

"Perhaps we're being too hard on him," said their aunt weakly, feeling that their uncle should have some defense. Robert Barton was a stern man, but usually a just one. She could not, however, by any stretch of the imagination, say that he had been kind.

"You know I'm not, Aunt!" he responded indignantly. "Just remember when Diana wished to go with Marian Stakeley and her family to the Lake District! Where was the harm in such a trip? But would he let her go? Absolutely not! And when I asked for the money to go fishing in Scotland with my friends from Cambridge, would he give it to me?"

"No," sighed his aunt. "And so, Trevor, you plan to speak with Appelby as soon as possible?"

"This very afternoon," he said firmly. "If Jenny will have me, by tonight I shall be an affianced man."

Diana and her aunt spent the afternoon in a flutter of excitement, fearful now of leaving the house in case they should miss Trevor's call to inform them how his suit had prospered. Aunt Lavinia was inclined to take a pessimistic view of the whole matter, certain that Robert Barton would indeed spoke Trevor's wheel and forbid him to marry, even if Lord Appelby gave his permission, which she assured Diana was by no means a certainty.

"Nonsense, Aunt!" Diana protested loyally. "Lord Appelby could have no reason to refuse such an eligible man as Trevor. After all, aside from being handsome and personable, he also has a title and he eventually *will* have a fortune, despite all Uncle Robert can do. And when Lord Appelby gives his consent, how can Uncle Robert possibly refuse?"

"Well, I certainly like your way of looking at it, my dear," conceded Lavinia, giving way as usual before Diana's youthful confidence.

"Because it's the proper way, Aunt," Diana informed her, grinning. "At any moment Trevor will bound in and give us the happy news."

When Trevor arrived, however, he did not bound. He looked instead like a soldier suffering from the shock of battle.

"What is it, Trevor?" demanded Diana, alarmed by his appearance. "Come sit down and tell us what's happened."

The two ladies guided him to the sofa, where he collapsed, his head in his hands.

"Didn't Lord Appelby give his permission, Trevor?" asked Diana, stroking his hair gently. "If not, you must try again, you know. You can't give up with just one attempt."

Trevor raised his head from his hands and stared at them bleakly. "You don't understand, Di," he said in a low voice. "There's no point in that. Appelby needs money. He told me that he likes me and he would give his permission in an instant if I had access to my fortune now."

"Then he's just the same as he's always been,"

commented Lavinia sadly, "the greatest spendthrift in the country."

"Did he say how much money he needed, Trev?" asked Diana, determined to find a way out of the dilemma.

"He needs a hundred thousand pounds by the end of the month," replied her brother in a low voice, once again burying his face in his hands.

Both of the ladies stared at him, horrified.

"Well, how will he get the money if he doesn't get it from you, Trevor?" asked Diana slowly, trying to think the matter through.

Once again he looked up, his dark eyes almost black against the abnormal pallor of his skin. "He will marry her to Lord Treffington."

"Treffington?" gasped his aunt. "Why, he must be seventy years old if he's a day!"

Trevor nodded and smiled humorlessly. "That may be true, but on the other hand, he has a hundred thousand pounds."

"Surely you're wrong, Trev!" said Diana. "A father wouldn't do that to his child. Surely you misunderstood!"

He shook his head. "There's no misunderstanding—and he will do it. The only hope he offered me is that he will wait a fortnight before giving Treffington his permission."

"But what good will that do you, Trevor?" asked his aunt. "It wouldn't matter if you had two years instead of two weeks."

"No! I *will* think of something, Aunt."

"Of course you will," said Diana reassuringly, holding his hand firmly. "And we will help you."

In her heart, however, she grieved for her brother. She could see no way that he could win his bride within the allotted time.

Despite the fact it was their first night in London, Diana had no heart now for an outing. She and her aunt ate quietly at home, and Lavinia went to bed early, pleading a headache. So it was that she was alone when, much to her surprise, Tom was shown into the drawing room.

"Why, Tom," she began, "what a pleasant surprise—" Then she saw his expression and stopped. "Has something happened to Trevor?" she asked, her heart in her throat.

"No, Di—that is, Lady Diana," he said hurriedly. "At least—well, something is happening to him right now and I don't know who else to go to. But Trevor is going to have my head for coming to you," he finished miserably, sinking into a chair.

"What's going on, Tom?" she demanded. "Where is Trevor? What's happening to him?"

Reluctantly he told her, and Diana hurried upstairs to get her things. "You must first take me home with you," she informed him when she came down, a small bag in her hand. "I need some things of Trevor's."

"To my lodgings?" he asked blankly. "That's not the proper thing to do, Di. What if someone sees us? They'd have the wrong idea and then Trevor really would have my head."

"Nonsense!" replied Diana firmly. "No one will see us and if they do, I'm just collecting some things for my brother. What could be more innocent than that?"

Recognizing from her tone that he had no choice in the matter, Tom escorted her unhappily to the lodgings that he and Trevor occupied together, and tried to ignore the lifted brows of his valet when they arrived. He could only be grateful that Gardiner, Trevor's valet, was absent for the evening.

Diana disappeared into Trevor's bedchamber, and when she emerged a few moments later, Tom leaped to his feet, his eyes almost starting from his head. Before him stood Diana, attired in immaculate gentlemen's evening dress, and looking almost exactly like her brother.

"You can't do this, Di!" he pleaded. "Think of what will happen if someone discovers you."

"No one will know who I am. I'll need one of the frieze greatcoats you told me about, Tom. I'll take yours—and the hat, too please. That will help to conceal my features and my hair. How very fortunate it is that you men wear such gear for your gambling."

Her unhappy companion looked as though he considered it anything but fortunate as he handed her the long, loose coat that lay on the chair beside him.

Diana's hair was caught up firmly in a tight coil at the back of her head, and the large straw hat that Tom reluctantly handed her concealed it nicely and shadowed her face. A cheerful wreath of daisies ringed the brim of the hat. That, she told herself, should give her confidence. Daisies had long been her favorite flower.

Although she could still see no way out of their problems, she was now determined to find a way.

Trevor was not to be sacrificed on the golden altar of fortune as long as she had a breath in her body.

"Well, let's go to Le Chauteau Royale, Tom," she said briskly. "Trevor has been alone there for too long a time as it is. He must be mad to think he can win a fortune gaming. He has no head for cards and his luck is always out."

Groaning, Tom followed her out the door, feeling that his own luck was quite out and trying not to think of what his friend's reaction to this charade was going to be. Escorting Trevor's sister into a notorious gambling hell was scarcely going to win his approval. Tom shuddered and decided it was best not to think about that until it was necessary.

Two

"What's happened, Trev? What's wrong?" whispered Diana, leaning close to her brother.

The candles lit the alcove brightly, and she was grateful for her wide-brimmed hat and for the potted palms that screened them from the view of the rest of the room. She and Tom had held their breath as they strolled up the stairs and past the crowded faro table, Diana doing her best to imitate Trevor's easy stride. To their relief they found him alone, although it was clear from the cards that had been dealt there was a game still in progress.

The young Earl of Landford raised his head from his arms and stared at her. "What are you doing here, Di?" he asked hoarsely, his eyes wide with disbelief. "This is no place for you."

"Nor for you," she murmured grimly, glancing about the smoke-filled room. "We must get you out of here at once."

"We? Who's with you?"

Tom cleared his throat unhappily. "I am, Trev. I really couldn't help it, you know," he added nervously, seeing his friend's outraged expression. "She was going to come no matter what I said, and I couldn't let her wander off alone to a gambling hell."

"No, no, of course you couldn't," agreed Trevor, his head sinking once again, not alert enough to ask how she came to know his whereabouts. "Just get her out of here now, Tom."

"Not without you, Trevor," said Diana firmly, taking an equally firm grip on his arm. "I came to take you home and I'm going to do it."

Her brother looked up at her desperately, his eyes red-rimmed and fearful. "I can't pay what I just lost to Melville," he whispered. "He's gone for champagne and I'm on my way to hell in a handbasket. I can't raise that kind of money."

"Give him your vowel. We will figure it out tomorrow when you're feeling more the thing," replied Diana.

"Tomorrow," echoed Tom hopefully. "Just the thing, Trev. A little rest and everything will look better."

"Don't be such a gudgeon!" snapped his friend. "Tomorrow won't make everything better! I'm finished! Jenny will marry Treffington, and at this rate I will already have lost my fortune before I even have it."

"Nonsense," replied his sister briskly. "Tom's right. Tomorrow we will think of how to put this to rights."

"Di, you have to leave! Melville will be back any moment! Tom, get her out of here!" he commanded his friend, who looked at him helplessly.

"I'm not going to leave unless you promise that you'll quit at the end of this hand and give Melville your vowel." Diana looked as distinctly mulish as it was possible for her to do, and her brother could see that he could easily have a scene on his hands if he resisted.

Trevor groaned and rubbed his eyes with his fists, as though he would be able to see more clearly afterwards. "All right, Di, all right! I'll do it—I can't think of anything else I *can* do."

"Fine. And promise that you'll come round tomorrow morning so that we can take care of this."

Her brother looked at her in disbelief. "Have your wits gone begging, Di?" he demanded. "I'll come round in the morning, but how can we possibly take care of this?"

He lowered his voice to a whisper so that no one else could hear. "I've lost almost eight thousand pounds, Di. Where can we get that kind of money? You know that Uncle Robert won't lift a hand to help me."

Diana felt her throat constrict for a moment, but she swallowed hard and her voice sounded natural when she spoke. "We don't need Uncle Robert, Trevor. We're clever enough to take care of this ourselves." For the moment she would not bring up the fact that trying to acquire the money by gambling— especially when one had no talent for it—scarcely came under the heading of clever behavior.

Despite his doubt, her calm assurance made Trevor sit up straight and look at her with a more hopeful expression. Tom, too began to look a little brighter. "Do you really think we can handle this?"

Diana nodded with an assurance she was far from feeling. "Absolutely. You just be certain that you finish this hand and leave immediately. Promise me, Trevor."

He lifted his right hand and managed a weak grin. "I swear," he responded. He looked her up and down, appearing to notice her costume for the first time. "I give you my word as one gentleman to another."

As Tom and Diana made their way toward the entrance, they encountered a man on the stairs. As they passed him, he glanced briefly at Diana, who had pulled her hat low over her eyes, and then looked back again sharply, but Tom nodded briefly at the man and hurried her on.

"Who was that?" she demanded in a whisper as the heavy mahogany door closed behind them.

"Jack Melville," replied Tom tersely, signaling for his tilbury to be brought up. "I never should have let Trevor come to a place like this. It's filled with men like Melville."

"How did he get that scar on his face?" Diana asked. He had looked much like her own vision of a pirate—tall, dark, elegantly dressed, a jagged scar creasing one cheek.

"A duel," he replied grimly. "Everyone knows that Melville is a dangerous man. You don't trifle with him. I can't think how Trev fell into his hands so quickly. By the time I found him here this evening, they were already engaged in play and I couldn't get him to break away. I am to blame for this."

Diana patted his arm comfortingly. "Of course you aren't, Tom. You tried to stop it and you came to get me. You've done all that you could."

Knowing what Trevor's opinion of pulling his sister into this would very likely be once he had an opportunity to think it over, Tom shook his head bleakly and helped her into the tilbury. As they rattled home through the silent streets, Diana considered the problem carefully.

"I know what to do," she announced finally.

Tom turned to her eagerly, but she shook her head. "I shan't explain it to you right now, Tom," she said, patting his hand, "but I know I shall need your help."

"What do you have in mind, Di?" he inquired a little apprehensively. He had known her for many years, and experience had taught him that her ideas sometimes involved considerable risk. "You know I'd give Trev the money in a minute if I could."

Again she patted his hand. "We both know that, Tom. Your funds are as firmly tied up as ours are, but I believe I've thought of a way around that. You find out exactly how much he has lost to Melville tonight and come round to see me first thing in the morning—and come without Trev. He'll probably not awaken before noon at any rate."

Tom had to be satisfied with that and, having seen her to her door, went home to await his unfortunate friend.

He appeared as early as was acceptable the next morning, eager to be of service to his friend. Lady Lavinia was still in bed, so they were able to meet privately.

"Did he get home all right last night, Tom?" she

asked anxiously as the butler closed the door to the drawing room.

He nodded. "But he was a wreck, Di. He had lost another five hundred pounds. It was all that Gardiner and I could do to get him to bed."

"I'm surprised that you could manage to do it. When he is upset, he usually paces and is up all hours of the night."

Tom looked a little embarrassed and regarded the cane in his hands seriously for a moment before replying. "Yes, I know. I had—well, I had Gardiner bring him a drink and I slipped a little laudanum into it—just enough to make him sleep."

He looked up at her anxiously and was relieved when she smiled approvingly. "Good for you, Tom! If you hadn't, he would still be up. As it is, we have time to begin our work."

Tom leaned forward eagerly. "You really do have something definite in mind then, Di? Tell me what I may do to help."

"First of all, Tom, do you know Melville's direction?"

He stared at her for a moment, then nodded. "Everyone knows that. He won Livingstone House from Terence Drake last fall. That house had belonged to the Drake family for six generations, but Melville won that and Drake's best hunters in one evening."

He paused and looked at her uneasily. "Why do you wish to know, Di?"

Without replying, Diana handed him a book that had been sitting on the table beside her.

Tom stared at it for a moment. "A book?" he said blankly. "Do you want me to read something?"

Diana shook her head and leaned across to open it. Instead of turning pages, she lifted a clasp and opened it, lifting the cover to reveal three velvet pouches.

"Why, it's not a book at all!" he exclaimed admiringly. "How clever an idea!"

Diana nodded in agreement. "My mother used it to carry her jewels in when she traveled. My grandmother was robbed once while she was in Paris, and she had this made to be able to keep her jewels in an inconspicuous place that a thief could easily miss."

Tom's admiration of the "book" faded as he remembered what they were doing.

"Why are you showing me this, Di?" he asked uncomfortably. "I thought that you were going to explain your plan."

"I am," she responded. "I know that there are places in London where one can take jewelry and be lent money for it. I—"

"Di!" Tom's eyebrows almost sailed completely out of sight. "How do you come to know about such things?"

She grinned at him, amused by his outraged expression. "Well, Tom, Trevor has been in scrapes before, so you know that I've heard about moneylenders. And then, of course, there's our neighbor in Leamington, Lady Clavell. She taught me about the value of jewels, and since she has had her own problems, she also told me about what one might expect in dealing with such people."

Tom groaned. "I can't be a party to this, Di. I can't let you sell your mother's jewelry."

"I'm not selling it. I have every intention of reclaiming it later," she replied calmly, closing the cover of the book and fastening it firmly.

"How?" he demanded.

"I'll worry about that later. Right now we have to take care of the most pressing problems. I want you to take the pieces I have in here and get the money to pay Melville. I think there should be more than enough here to do that and I have a plan for that extra money."

"What is it?" demanded Tom suspiciously. "I shouldn't think it would be enough to pay Lord Appelby."

"Of course not. That's not what it's for—not directly, at any rate."

"And what does that mean?" he asked, growing nervous now.

"I'll explain it to you when you bring me back the money, Tom. Do be quick about it, though. Aunt Lavinia will sleep later than usual because of our trip, but she won't stay in bed all morning, and I don't want to have to explain things to her just yet."

Tom groaned. "I should think not!" He looked at her miserably. "I really cannot do this for you, Di. Your aunt and your brother would roast me alive."

Di rose and picked up the jewelry box. "I understand your predicament, Tom," she said kindly. "And I'm not angry with you."

"Then you're giving up that notion?" he asked

eagerly, his eyes alight with the hope of reprieve as he rose with her.

She shook her head. "Naturally not. I have to have the money for my plan. I shall pawn the jewels myself."

Tom sank back onto the sofa. "And if I allowed you to do that, they would roast me alive only after cutting out my liver." He looked at her and smiled a little. "I haven't talked like that since we were schoolchildren."

He stood up again and squared his shoulders, then put out his hand for the jewels. "I will be as quick as it's possible to be," he assured her. "I just pray that I don't have to explain myself to Trev and your aunt immediately."

"I'll take care of that, Tom," she assured him, kissing him on the cheek so that he flushed brightly. "What you're doing is for Trev's own good, you know, and that must be your comfort."

He nodded and walked briskly to the door, telling himself firmly that he must not think about this matter too much or he would fall into such a fit of the dismals that he would belong on the stage like Mrs. Siddons in one of her tragedies. He found, however, that he could not avoid feeling a slight discomfort in the area of his torso where he imagined his liver to be.

When he returned, Lady Lavinia had not yet put in an appearance and Diana was waiting for him eagerly, pulling him into the drawing room before the offended butler could even announce him.

"How much did you get, Tom?" she demanded in a low voice as he handed the "book" back to her.

He opened the clasp of the box and pointed. "Ten thousand pounds," he said quietly.

Once again she kissed him, then hurriedly counted out the amount due to Melville. "I have to leave you alone for a moment, but I'll be back down directly, Tom, just as soon as I write a note to go with this. I'll have Tibbett bring you a brandy."

Before he could protest that it was too early for him to be drinking anything other than coffee, she was opening the door. "I'll be back directly," she told him cheerfully. "And thank you again, Tom. Now we have enough money to carry out the rest of the plan."

Before he could inquire into the meaning of this statement, she had closed the door behind her, and he was left to meditate upon what seemed to him the distinctly ominous meaning of her words. He patted his midsection in an attempt to calm his liver. When Tibbett appeared in a few moments bearing a decanter of brandy, Tom allowed him to pour a glass, drank it briskly, and was just considering the possibility of a fortifying second glass as Diana reappeared.

She smiled widely as she sat down next to him. "I just sent the footman to Melville's home with the money, Tom. I gave him a guinea to do it, so I don't think there's much fear that he will mention it to any of the other servants so that Aunt Lavinia eventually discovers it. He is just hired for the season and he doubtless thinks I have a *tendre* for that awful man. I don't want to tell Aunt about this until we have everything well in hand."

Tom shuddered as he thought of Lady Lavinia's

very justifiable distress should she become aware of the situation. His thoughts then turned immediately to the fears that he had been entertaining during her absence, and reluctantly he asked, "Di, just what did you mean when you referred to 'the rest of the plan'? How are you going to use the rest of the money?"

Diana stared at him, her dark eyes as innocent as possible. "Why, to win back the money for my jewelry and that needed for Lord Appelby, of course."

Tom blanched visibly and she saw in amazed sympathy that small beads of perspiration were beginning to form on his downy upper lip. "How can we possibly do that, Di?" he asked, hoping that his voice didn't sound as weak as he feared it did.

"I'm certain that Trevor told Melville that he was a master of écarté and piquet," she replied, ignoring Tom's puzzled look at her apparently irrelevant observation.

Unfortunately, however, he was soon able to discern the reason for her comment.

"I cannot imagine why he fancies himself such an exceptional card player," she continued. "You know, yourself, Tom, that he has no head for it. I, on the other hand, play exceedingly well."

Tom nodded, still puzzled. "Yes, he has always said that you play very well for a girl."

She sniffed. "What he means by that is that he always loses when we play. Why, there was no one at the Leamington assemblies that could best me."

Tom's expression grew apprehensive, and a less determined heart than hers might have softened. He looked like a hare cornered by hounds.

"But what good will that do us?" he asked, his throat dry and his voice growing thinner.

"I sent a note to Melville, along with the money," she replied in a very businesslike voice. She could see that she would have to provide the steadiness of nerve for their operation.

"A note?" he echoed piteously.

Diana nodded. "Now, Tom, it is your business to be certain that Trevor doesn't return to that hell tonight."

"I should say that he won't!" he exclaimed, momentarily diverted as he felt himself upon firmer ground. "Why, the very idea!"

"You see, Tom, I'll be there dressed as Trev, and it would be most unfortunate to have both of us there at the same time. The only thing that saved us last night was that their table was screened from view and that I was there for so very brief a time."

Tom was striving valiantly to maintain both his dignity and his emotional balance, but it must be observed that he made several small gobbling sounds before he managed to speak. "What are you talking about, Di?" he gasped. "You can't go to that place! What do you expect to do?"

"Just what I've told you," she replied calmly. "I plan to win a considerable amount of money, and I've arranged to meet Melville at eleven o'clock tonight."

"At Le Chateau Royale?"

She nodded. "At Le Chateau Royale."

"You must be mad, Diana!" Tom's voice regained its strength as the full horror of the situation dawned upon him. "Aside from the fact that you won't win a farthing because Melville never loses, just think of the consequences if he discovers you're not Trev! And what if he discovers you're a woman—a woman disguised as a man in a gambling hell! Your reputation will be ruined before you are even introduced to society!"

Diana shrugged. "That's no great matter to me, Tom. I've done very nicely without society thus far, and Trevor needs money if he is to marry his Jenny."

"And what if I can't keep him away from Le Chateau tonight?" demanded Tom, changing his tactics. "What if he goes in spite of what I say?"

"Well, Tom," she replied patiently, "if before the two of you leave home tonight you mix a little laudanum in his drink—just as you so cleverly did last night—he will be fast asleep in no time. It's a great convenience that you and Trevor decided to share an establishment," she added with satisfaction.

"I gave him the laudanum last night for his own good!" Tom protested.

"Well, this would be for his own good, too, Tom. Aren't we doing this for him?"

"But deliberately drug his drink to trick him? I'll do no such thing, Diana Ballinger! You must think I have rats in my upper works!" Feeling that justice was on his side, Tom's voice was growing stronger once more.

She patted his arm soothingly. "Not at all, Tom. I think that you are the best of friends and that you want to help Trevor."

"Well, naturally I wish to help Trev, but—"

"And you want to go with me to Le Chateau Royale so that I don't make a misstep while I'm there—

because you know I shall go, whether you come with me or not."

Tom again turned pale and collapsed on the sofa. He knew himself to be outmaneuvered, and he tried not to imagine all the things that could go wrong that evening.

Knowing that she had him where she wanted him, Diana ruthlessly delivered the *coup de grâce*.

"And I hesitated to mention it earlier, Tom, because it seems so melodramatic, but—"

She hesitated a moment and Tom watched her nervously, trying to keep from falling into his childhood habit of biting his nails when under duress. The word "melodramatic" immediately conjured up dozens of horrible images that played through his mind one after another as he waited for her to speak.

Diana lowered her voice and looked around cautiously, even though they were alone in the room. "You have seen how extremely distraught Trevor has been since learning that Jenny might marry Lord Treffington."

Tom nodded.

"He has always been highly strung, of course— much different in temperament from me," she continued.

Tom mentally endorsed this observation with great earnestness. So far as he could see, they might look alike and both were high-spirited and merry, but apart from that, they were worlds apart in disposition. The present state of his liver could attest to that. He had not fully realized just how different until the present moment, and he resolved that hereafter he would be more observant of those about him and avoid traps like the one that was presently closing upon him.

Diana leaned toward him confidingly and dropped her voice still further. "I have never seen him like this for more than an hour at a time, Tom. He is so sunk in despair that I fear he might do something desperate."

Tom stared at her, quite wild-eyed by now. "But he already has, Diana, he has! Just think of his gambling away eight thousand pounds last night! That's desperate if anything is!"

"Yes, of course, it is, Tom," she returned, trying not to let any irritation show in her voice at his failure to follow the implication of her words. "But what I mean is that—that he might try to do some damage to himself."

Tom could not have looked more horrified if his long deceased grandfather had appeared next to him on the sofa. His eyes fairly bulged from his head, and he reached for the decanter of brandy to pour himself another glass.

"Just see how reasonable my plan is," Diana observed comfortingly, pouring the drink for him. "Tonight Trevor will be home having a good rest to steady his nerves with Gardiner watching over him, and you and I will be doing our best to make it possible for him to marry Jenny."

Tom, who was thinking more along the lines of reading in the latest scandal sheet about the unavoidable disaster he saw lying ahead of them, bolted his drink just as the door opened and Trevor entered.

"I say, Tom, it's rather early in the day to be drinking, don't you think? Hardly the example to set for Di," observed Trevor disapprovingly. "At any rate, I don't see what's driving you to the bottle. I'm the one that should be drowning my sorrows."

Feeling ill-equipped to talk with anyone just then, Tom stood up, bowed to them both, and tottered toward the door without replying. Trevor looked after him in amazement.

"Do you think we should let him go out?" he asked Diana in a low voice. "He looks all about in his head to me, and I've never known Tom to take a drink in the morning."

His sister shook her head decisively. "No, he's just overcome by the knowledge that you have been able to reclaim your voucher from Melville."

He looked at it without saying a word. "How did that happen, Di?" he finally managed to say.

"Do you remember our second cousin, Elvira Dalton, that we met once when she passed through Leamington on her way to London?"

Trevor nodded.

"I had not told you because it happened so recently, but just before we left home, I received a letter from her lawyer announcing that she had left me eight thousand pounds in her will," Diana continued, disposing of Elvira, who was still thriving in Chester, without a qualm. "I went directly to his place of business yesterday afternoon and picked it up. I had planned to use part of it to defray our expenses here, but your need is greater."

He looked at her, too stunned to speak.

"After last night I knew, of course, what I must do, and I sent round the money to Melville's home."

"How did you know his direction?" Trevor asked at last.

"Tom told me," she responded brightly, glancing at her victim, who had frozen in the doorway and was watching her helplessly. Trevor turned to stare at him, but the hapless Tom fled before he could be questioned.

Three

Seeing that he had no recourse, Tom did just as Diana wished. He had given his own valet the evening off, and he had asked Gardiner to stay at Trevor's bedside for the evening since he did not appear to be well. The dose of laudanum had made the victim pale, so Tom's story was quite believable, and Gardiner took his post with alacrity.

Having taken these elementary precautions to ensure privacy, he awaited her arrival with considerable trepidation. Lord Ralston had never been noted for his courage in the face of danger, but he was looking it in the eye now, knowing that he had no choice. He laid out one of Trevor's evening outfits in his own chamber and, having done all he could for the moment, sat down and waited for the sound of Diana's arrival.

It came all too soon, and after she had changed, he was once again confronted with a shadow image of Trevor.

"May I borrow your hat and your frieze coat again, Tom?" she inquired.

He nodded sadly, pointing toward a nearby chair. "I knew you would want them, so I ordered fresh daisies."

"Thank you, Tom, they look delightful. Daisies are always so cheerful!"

She smiled at him as brightly as if they were setting off for an evening at the opera, he thought dismally. It would take far more than the sight of a few daisies to cheer him up.

Together they set off for Le Chateau Royale, Tom reminding himself with every turn of the tilbury's wheels that he was indeed Lord Ralston, not some feckless schoolboy. He would not chew his fingernails nor fall into a fit—nor would he think of his midsection, which was aching suspiciously. He had a responsibility that he must meet.

"It's exciting, isn't it, Tom?" he heard Diana saying, as though from a great distance.

"Yes," he responded as promptly as possible, reminding himself again of his responsibility. "Indeed it is, Diana. Words fail me when I try to tell you how exciting it is." That much at least was true, he reflected miserably.

All too soon they arrived in front of Le Chateau Royale, and it was with difficulty that Tom reminded himself that he must not attempt to help Diana from the tilbury nor in any way indicate that she was not a man. Taking a deep breath, he turned toward the door, hearing her light step behind him.

They were quickly admitted and ushered to a small room on the third floor. Melville had been very busy with his arrangements, Tom reflected uncomfortably. No doubt he was looking forward to plucking his pigeon at least once more. He cast a hasty glance at Diana beside him. She showed no hint of the panic that was threatening to overtake him.

"Lord Ralston, what a pleasant surprise," murmured Melville, opening the door to them. "I had no idea that Lord Landford would be bringing company, but I am, naturally, delighted."

Tom bowed somewhat stiffly. "Thank you, sir. I was pleased that my friend wished for my company for the evening. I'm certain that you understand."

Melville regarded them both with some amusement. "I believe that I do, Lord Ralston. I'm certain that Lord Landford wished for moral support. It's not to be wondered at. The only thing that has caught me by surprise is the fact that Lord Landford wished to play again."

"Of course, he does, Mr. Melville," said Tom firmly, before Diana could speak.

Melville noted the flash in Landford's eyes at this liberty, and smiled to himself. Landford had seemed at first nothing more than a green lad, one that it was too easy to take advantage of. He had been surprised that the stripling was able to pay his debt so quickly—and that he had asked for another game. Now another stripling had clearly appointed himself the watchdog and had come to oversee the proceedings. This promised to be far more amusing than he had anticipated. To come out money ahead as well as to find himself amused was more than Melville expected of life these days. He had been bored for longer than he could remember.

Watching the pair before him from beneath lowered lids as he appeared to be giving his entire attention to shuffling the cards, he wondered just what desperation had brought this youngster and his companion back into his clutches. Whatever it was,

Melville admired the steadiness of his hands and his quiet, understated manner. It was with considerable surprise—and even more amusement—that he realized that Landford was studying him just as carefully. The boy's thick lashes partially concealed his gaze, but now and then he caught the unmistakable sparkle of a bright, intelligent, and very watchful eye.

"Well, Landford," he drawled, leaning back in his chair after half an hour of steady play, a pair of parentheses seeming to enclose his lips as he restrained an unaccustomed smile, "are you assessing my technique? Do I have some idiosyncrasy that indicates when I am holding a winning hand? Do I perhaps then hold them closer to my chest— as I believe you do—in order to protect myself?"

To his delight, the boy gasped slightly and his startled gaze rose momentarily to meet Melville's, but he was almost instantly in control of himself again. Obviously, he realized that he had just done precisely what Melville had described. Nonetheless, he coolly laid down his cards and glanced back at his opponent.

"I believe, sir, that this would be an ideal moment for a break," said Diana, rising from the table. "I find myself growing quite stiff. May I bring you a glass as I return?"

Melville inclined his head slightly. "As you wish, Landford. Have you no objection to leaving me alone with the cards?" he inquired curiously as Ralston rose to accompany his friend.

Diana paused a moment and glanced back at her opponent in surprise. "Certainly not, sir. Would you have any such objection if the situation were reversed?"

Melville bowed. "Naturally not." As the other two left the room, he was left to reflect upon their naiveté—or at least upon that of Landford. Ralston had looked as though he thought Melville had made a legitimate point, and had glanced with some concern at the cards lying face down on the table; but it had been equally obvious that he was determined to accompany his friend.

Curiously enough, he found Landford's behavior more alert and self-confident than it had been the night before. In battle, he had seen young men who seemed high-strung and restive, like Landford had been last night, grow steady when they were faced with the possibility of death. An odd thing that had always seemed to him, that their courage should appear under fire. He rather admired the boy for facing him again.

He sat musing thus as he waited for them, wondering again why Ralston found it necessary to go when he had appeared to doubt the wisdom of leaving him alone with the hand that had already been dealt to Landford. After all, Ralston had not remained by his friend's side when they were playing last night. He had, in fact, disappeared before the evening was half over.

Suddenly he remembered last night's encounter on the stairs. He had thought for a moment that Landford was running away, but then he had found the boy exactly where he had left him. And he had realized that the frieze coat he wore was a slightly different shade from that of the young man he had seen with Ralston on the stairs. And Landford's hat had been garlanded with yellow roses, while the other wore daisies around the crown of his hat and a small bunch of daisies in his lapel. Too, he had not really seen the face of Ralston's companion clearly.

Doubtless he had thought it Landford simply because he had expected him to be with Ralston and because they were similar in size. Or perhaps after seeing him on the stairs the boy had hurried back to his place at the table, Melville himself having stopped along the way to speak with another of his recently plucked pigeons to remind him of the need to reclaim his vowel. But why would the boy have changed his coat and hat?

Just then the door opened and Landford and Ralston rejoined him. Landford was wearing a wreath of daisies on his hat and daisies in his lapel.

Diana looked across the table at her opponent and saw him gazing at her with uncomfortable intensity, his green eyes glittering. Were they glittering with greed, she wondered. If so, he would have a rude awakening. Thus far she was holding her own, and she had every intention of winning tonight.

"Is there something amiss, sir?" she asked briskly, growing restive under his gaze.

"Not at all, Landford," he drawled. "I was just admiring the daisies. They are quite delightful, you know." He did not know what game the boy was playing, but it was becoming quite entertaining.

Diana plucked one from her lapel and tossed it across the table to him. "By all means enjoy them more closely, Mr. Melville," she returned. "Shall we continue the game?"

Melville picked up the daisy, examined it with exaggerated interest, and then tucked it into his own lapel. "With the greatest of pleasure, sir," he drawled, picking up his own hand once more.

Diana, watching him through her eyelashes, saw that he was smiling, the scar on his cheek deepening and his white teeth flashing against his dark skin. When Tom left them a few minutes later to procure refreshments of a more substantial nature than champagne, he smiled again.

"You have a very devoted friend in Lord Ralston," he observed, rearranging his cards carefully.

"Yes, I have been most fortunate to have a loyal friend like Tom," agreed Diana absently, absorbed in studying her own hand.

"Loyal for the moment," returned Melville carelessly, "but only so long as it costs him nothing."

Diana flushed hotly and forgot her cards for a moment, glaring at her opponent. "You are wrong, Mr. Melville," she snapped. "Tom has been a good friend for years! You have no right to make such a remark!"

Melville shrugged. "I daresay he has. After all, what sacrifice has he been called upon to make for you—or you for him? It is then that you will discover that friendship and love—yes, even love—" he assured her, catching her startled glance, "is a matter of convenience. So long as all goes well, affection remains. Once trouble comes, or the wish to indulge one's own desires, affection flies out the window."

"How very cynical you are, sir," remarked Diana,

studying him. "You must have had a most unhappy life to make such an observation. I am sorry for it."

It was her opponent's turn to study her sharply. "I have no need of your sympathy," Melville assured her coldly. "I am sorry, though, for the disillusionment that lies ahead of you." And to his surprise, he discovered that it was true. He was rather sorry for the boy, still so trusting in his outlook.

At that moment the faithful Tom reappeared, bearing a plate of oddly assorted food: scalloped oysters, spring peas, pineapple, and lobster. Diana thanked him cordially and instructed him to sit down and make himself comfortable, and by all means to partake of the refreshments that he had brought, guessing correctly that Tom—unlike herself—was starving.

Melville, having refused all offers of refreshment himself, smiled as he watched Tom making his way steadily through the food he had procured for Landford.

"I am pleased to see that Lord Ralston will be able to keep body and soul together until the end of the evening."

Tom stared at him blankly, but Diana shook her head, smiling. "That dainty plate will never be enough, since Tom has not yet dined today. I am afraid that I interfered with his plans."

Tom began to protest, but Diana waved a hand of dismissal in his direction. "Nonsense, Tom. Go back and refill your plate. You know that you are longing to do so."

Realizing that he was indeed ravenous and that Diana appeared to be in no imminent danger, Tom took her advice and returned to replenish his supplies, leaving the other two to talk more comfortably.

"You wrong him, Mr. Melville," said Diana as Tom disappeared into the next room. "He is a kindly soul and the best of friends."

Melville looked at her thoughtfully, then nodded. "I hope for your sake that you are right, but I am afraid that a rude awakening lies ahead for you if he is put to the test. People don't sacrifice well, you know, no matter what your governess taught you."

Diana thought of the present sacrifice Tom was making and grinned. "I do wish, Mr. Melville, that you could be privy to some of the details of our relationship. Perhaps you might look with greater kindness upon Lord Ralston."

"Do tell me, sir. I am anxious to hear them," Melville assured her, smiling with unaccustomed warmth. Tom hurried back to her side at that precise moment and observed the smile, which he did not regard as a warm one.

"He looked exactly like a crocodile," Tom told her later as they were discussing the events of the evening on their way home. "Saw one once when I was just a tyke. A damned unnerving experience it was. The croc looked as though he could gobble you up with one bite. Just like Melville could have gobbled you up tonight."

"But he didn't, did he?" Diana returned comfortably, patting the pocket of her coat. "I won five hundred pounds from him tonight, Tom. There's nothing shabby about that—and the croc didn't sink his teeth into me."

"No," replied Tom uncomfortably, "but you can't

meet him again tomorrow night as you said you would, Di."

She stared at him. "Naturally I must meet him again, Tom. After all, it's only gentlemanly to allow him a chance to win his money back—except that I won't do any such thing, of course." She smiled confidently. "I am going to win again and Trevor will have his money sooner than he thinks."

"I won't drug him again to keep him at home, Di!" he protested. "Trev would know for certain that something was amiss!"

"Of course he would," Diana replied. "He isn't addle-pated. Your duty for the evening will be to keep him away from Le Chateau."

Tom sat bolt upright and stared at her, his eyes wide with horror. "I can't allow you to go to that place alone, Di! It was bad enough to have you there while I was with you every minute, but alone?"

"But you saw that there was no problem," she pointed out reasonably, "and Melville appears to present no real difficulty."

"No real difficulty?" he gasped. "You haven't the least notion what a man like that is capable of."

"Perhaps not, but I'm not afraid, Tom," she said calmly. "I shall go there again and win a little more money. Soon enough, we shall have good news for Trevor."

She did not add that she was looking forward to the next encounter with Jack Melville. She had found him oddly attractive, perhaps in part because, as Tom had pointed out repeatedly, he was a dangerous man.

It was more than that, however. He was an intelligent man, very quick-witted and with a sense of humor that had a bitter edge. Diana had not met anyone quite like him before, but she had felt quite certain as they played and talked that he was equally drawn to her. They had achieved an unusual sort of rapport during the course of the evening, and she looked forward to continuing it.

Tom sank back on his seat, trying to devote his attention to his team and to keep his mind off the horrible possibilities that the future held in store for him, not least of which was Trevor calling him out to avenge the honor of his sister. Perhaps he could ask Melville to act as his second, Tom thought miserably. Certainly none of his other friends would take up his cause. He would be a social pariah, the man who had aided in the ruin of Lady Diana Ballinger, an innocent young lady fresh from the country. People would point at him and stare. Sadly he envisioned his future as a hermit in some far corner of the country, where he would commune with crows and foxes that would not upbraid him for his failure to protect a lady.

Four

Tom was not allowed to repine long. He discovered all too quickly that the worst had not yet befallen him. Early the next morning he once again presented himself at Diana's home, hoping against hope that there had been a change in her plans.

"As a matter of fact, Tom, I have had a change of heart," she informed him cheerfully, pouring tea for both of them in the comfortable library.

Tom's normally rosy face glowed even more brightly at this happy news. Setting his cup carefully back in the saucer, he looked at her gratefully. "I knew that you would think better of your plan, Di," he said gratefully, allowing himself to lean back comfortably instead of sitting on the edge of his seat as he had been. "You're far too sensible a young lady to go to such a place again."

Diana nodded in earnest agreement. "You're quite correct, of course, Tom. I really had no desire to go to that gaming house again, but of course we have to think of Trevor."

Tom found himself nodding in agreement—a dangerous reaction, as he discovered all too quickly. He lifted the cup to his lips and enjoyed the first swallow of the fragrant brew, envisioning his old life as a respected member of society—and his prospects for the future—returning to him.

Diana leaned forward and patted his knee confidingly. "How much better it is now, Tom. Going to Melville's house is ever so much better than going to a public place. Imagine my excitement when I received his note this morning, suggesting that we play at his home tonight!"

Tom choked in a most ungentlemanly manner, splattering tea to such an extent that Diana was compelled to use two linen napkins to mop up the mess.

"You can't mean that, Di!" he protested, finally able to speak again. He scrubbed his cravat violently but without any awareness that he was doing so, quite completing its ruin. "You cannot go to the house of such a man! I forbid it!"

There was a sudden silence as Diana eyed him, and he realized that his choice of words had been most unfortunate. Blushing, he hurried once more into speech.

"Di, you know that I haven't any right to forbid you to do anything, but—do think about this. What would happen if people discovered that you had been alone with him in his home—and dressed as a man, to boot! Your name would be on the lips of every scandal-monger in the *ton*! And Trev would call me out once he knew that I knew you were going to do it and didn't stop you! And what's more, I wouldn't blame him for doing so!"

Overcome, he buried his face in a tea-stained napkin while Diana stroked his hair comfortingly.

"Come now, Tom," she said soothingly. "Trev knows that there is no reasoning with me and that you wouldn't have had the least prospect of changing my mind once I had determined to do this. He won't hold you responsible for my actions. Don't take this so much to heart."

"How can I not, Di?" he protested. "Even if Trev would forgive me, how could I forgive myself?" He stood up abruptly, almost oversetting the tea tray. He looked quite wild, his carefully brushed locks now standing in spikes because of Diana's comforting fingers as well as his own distressed rumpling.

The door opened and Trevor strolled in, the picture of sartorial perfection, the pride of his valet. The earl might be hollow-eyed and slightly gaunt, but he was immaculate despite his breaking heart. He stared at his friend in amazement, taking in the ruin of his cravat and waistcoat and the disarray of his hair.

"I say, Tom," he said in some distress. "Is there something amiss? You haven't seemed at all yourself for the past two days."

Tom stared at his friend, then at Diana. "I assure you, Trevor, that I am perfectly fine. If you will both excuse me, I have an urgent appointment that I must keep." And bowing stiffly to both of them, he turned and made his way blindly toward the door.

"I shall be back directly, Trev," Diana murmured in a low voice as she followed their friend out the door.

"Tom," she whispered, catching his arm before he could make his way to the door that the footman was holding wide for him. "Tom, stop and talk to me a moment."

Reluctantly, Tom turned to her, feeling like a hapless insect struggling in the web of a most determined spider.

"Tom, I shall be quite all right tonight," she whispered, drawing him to her side. "You know that Melville keeps a large establishment with servants everywhere. I learned as much from the footman who took Trevor's money to him."

He looked at her earnestly. "But what's to assure us that they will be present in full force tonight, Di?" he returned, whispering too and feeling like a miscreant. "What would you do if you needed help?"

"Tom, remember that I shall not be Diana tonight. I shall be the Earl of Landford. I shan't stand in any need of help." She caught his arm as he turned to walk away. "And if I did need help, Tom, I know that I could always send for you."

He flushed in gratification, forgetting for the moment that she would have no idea how to find him if he was busy keeping Trevor occupied. "And I would be there in a moment," he replied, patting her hand reassuringly.

"I know that you would be," she returned. "And remember, Tom," she added, "Trev will forgive us anything if we are successful. If he has his Jenny, then all of this distress will have been worthwhile."

Tom nodded. She was quite right, of course. That was one of the most unsettling things about Diana. Her motives were usually unquestionably correct when she asked you to do things that you had no intention of doing and that were damnably uncomfortable, but you did them because you felt that she was in the right of things.

"And can you send your mother's carriage to wait for me at the corner at ten?" she asked in a low voice. It was most convenient that Tom's mother greatly preferred the country but left her home in town fully staffed. Tom had refused to live there, desiring to live for a while with Trevor and have his independence from servants who had known him since he was in leading-strings, and his mother had agreed, always assuring him that anything needed at Ralston House was naturally his to command.

Seeing no way out of it and comforting himself that she at least would be protected on her way to and from Melville's home, he nodded.

Once the door had closed securely behind him, she returned to the drawing room, where Trevor was frowning with terrible intensity at the silver teapot.

"What's wrong with him, Di?" he demanded as she closed the door behind her. "Tom has always been the calmest and most levelheaded of any of my friends, but for the past two days he has acted like another man. What do you think is wrong with him?"

Diana took a deep breath. Tom would forgive her in time—particularly if he never learned the full details of her perfidy.

"He has been very distressed, Trev," she said, drawing her brother down beside her on the sofa. "You must know that he would do anything to be of service to you." That much at least was entirely truthful, she thought with satisfaction.

Trevor nodded and she continued. "He is afraid that you will gamble your fortune away and that he will not be able to prevent your doing so," she said, looking her brother full in the eye. "He considers your well-being—and keeping you away from gambling—as his responsibility."

"But how am I to win Jenny?" protested Trevor, rising from his seat. "I don't have any secret means, so I must gamble if I am to keep her from Treffington."

Diana took his arm firmly and pulled him back down beside her. "Trev, you saw Tom just now, didn't you?" she demanded.

He nodded uncomfortably.

"Well? And are you quite willing to be responsible for what happens if you go out gambling tonight when he feels it is his duty to stop you?"

Her brother stared at her, unwilling to commit himself, but she wouldn't allow him to take the easy way out.

"Answer me, Trev!" she said firmly. "Are you willing to be responsible for poor Tom's condition if he isn't able to keep you from gambling? Would you wish to go down and identify his body if he plunged into the Thames after you lost another small fortune?"

"Good God, no!" Trevor exclaimed, revolted by the very thought that he would sacrifice his friend's life. "You know, Di, that I would never allow any harm to come to Tom because of me!"

She nodded in satisfaction. "That's what I thought, Trevor. It will be your duty tonight to keep him from doing anything desperate. Make him feel that he is protecting you, that he is keeping you from any possible harm." She stared at him for a moment. "Are you able to do that?"

Her brother nodded indignantly. "Well, of course I am! Good Lord, you know that I'd do anything for old Tom after all he's been to me over the years!"

Diana threw her arms around him. "I knew that I could count on you to keep him from coming to harm," she said gratefully. "You can tell me tomorrow morning just how things go tonight. I know that I can trust you with Tom's well-being."

Trevor nodded firmly. "Of course, you can, Di. After all, if Tom can't place his confidence in me, then what sort of world has this come to be?"

Diana smiled at him. This was all turning out much better than she had dared hope. Aunt Lavinia was once again still asleep, Trevor was determined to protect Tom, and Tom was equally determined to protect Trevor. She would be left free to take care of Mr. Jack Melville and to discover precisely the source of his attraction. Perhaps it was the air of danger about him, or perhaps it was the challenge he presented. Whatever the reason, he made her feel curiously alive, and she found herself in the happy position of doing something that she felt to be both necessary and pleasurable.

Standing in front of her mirror that night, she tried a variety of ways of doing her cravat and of sweeping her dark hair into place. She wished, of course, to look convincing, but she also hoped that she would look devastatingly attractive. She could think of no reason to show Jack Melville any mercy whatsoever.

Five

Her quarry had been looking forward to the evening with equal pleasure. He had ordered the finest of champagnes, the most choice hors d'oeuvres. The Earl of Landford, he felt certain, would appreciate the finest that he could provide. No matter what game the boy was playing, he would not, at least, be able to accuse his host of being niggardly in his provisions for the evening.

Melville had checked and double-checked the refreshments, drawing considerable astonishment from his butler by his attention to details that had never before mattered to him. And he had further amazed his staff by his instructions, insisting that he should be waited upon only by his valet, his most trusted servant, and only by that gentleman as he should be summoned by a bell. His staff was astounded, but willing. Melville was a very demanding, but very generous, master. Whatever he required, he would have.

As Melville paced the length of his library, where the two of them would spend the evening, he pondered the information that he had learned about his young guest. The reason for the earl's desperate need for money had come to his attention that day at White's. He had been idly reading the paper when Basil Stepping, a notorious gossip, had come in and made himself comfortable on a nearby sofa.

"Well, Appelby is in the suds again," he had remarked cheerfully to two of his friends, ordering a drink from a grave waiter who had appeared instantly.

"What, being towed up the River Tick, is he?" inquired one of them. "Scarcely a news item, old man."

"No, he may be all to pieces again, but he won't pay the piper," remarked Stepping. "His daughter will, though. Poor girl," he added as an afterthought.

"What? Is he marrying her off?" asked his friend, showing a little more interest. "She isn't much more than out of the schoolroom, is she?"

Before Stepping could answer, the other friend nodded. "But perhaps it isn't such a bad thing," he observed. "I saw her with young Landford at Sally Jersey's rout the other evening. The chit could do far worse than Landford, you know, and the two of them were smelling of April and May if ever any couple was."

At this point the conversation had Melville's full attention. Stepping had snorted and leaned back more comfortably into the sofa. "The boy won't be marrying her," he informed them, eager to see the effect of his next words. "I have it on good authority that old Treffington is sure of her."

The other two gasped. "Why, that old reprobate has to be fifty years older than the girl if he's a day!"

exclaimed one. "Appelby isn't such a monster as to do that to his own flesh and blood!"

Stepping gazed at his friends, enjoying his moment. There was nothing he prized so highly as being the first with a particularly delectable bit of gossip.

"Remember that we're speaking of Appelby," he reminded them. "Of course he would sell her off if the need were great enough—and it obviously is. The girl is a toothsome bit and she has caught Treffington's fancy."

"Well, why not marry her to Landford?" inquired one of the others reasonably. "My father knew his and he says that the family is as rich as Croesus. I should think Appelby would snap up the boy in an instant. Thought so the instant I saw him dancing with Lady Genevieve."

Stepping, better informed than his friend, had shaken his head. "Landford can't touch his money for another four years without his guardian's approval, and what fool would let him fall into Appelby's clutches?"

The three of them had sat for some time, speculating upon the possible date of the nuptials and the methods that Appelby might use to put as good a face as possible upon the sale of his daughter. Their pity for the girl had been real enough, but it had disappeared in their enjoyment of the gossip.

When the other two had left, Melville had plucked a few more interesting bits of information from the willing Stepping. He had learned, for instance, that the young earl had a sister.

"I've met the young man, but I wasn't aware that

he had a sister. Is she in town with him?" Melville
had inquired casually.

Stepping shook his head. "Buried in the country
somewhere," he observed. "My father said there's
an uncle that holds the purse strings. He probably
keeps the sister locked up tight so that she won't
run off with some half-pay officer."

All in all, his afternoon at the club had been most
profitable. Certain that Landford was trying desperately to make enough money to marry Appelby's
daughter, Melville could almost feel sorry for the
boy—but not quite. His own experience had taught
him that love was a nonexistent commodity, and that
Landford might as well be disillusioned now as later.
He had told the boy as much last night about his
friendship with young Ralston.

Even were he to marry Lady Genevieve, he would
no doubt discover in short order that the girl was
not what he had thought her to be, and he would
regret having made his choice at so young and im-
pressionable an age, when he still believed that a
sustained love was possible. With that in mind,
Melville felt almost as though he were Landford's
benefactor by keeping him from winning the young
woman. At least he would be able to retain his illusions for a little longer.

Melville himself had been burnt by his association
with women, if you counted more than romantic affairs of the heart. His own mother, the delightful
but decadent Lady Sarah Melville, the third daughter of the Duke of Sommerfield, had had a secure
hold upon the affections of her only son. She had
not been a particularly kind or maternal woman,

but she had held young Jack in thrall. Her beauty and her casually playful manner had early won his heart, and he had not noticed then that her manner was much the same with everyone, including the footmen, one of whom she had run away with when Jack was only nine.

His bitterness had been as great as that of his father, who had always been a cold and distant man. Marshall Melville's pride had been severely wounded both by his wife's very public defection and by the fact that she had chosen a mere servant as her consort. He had forbidden everyone, including his son, to mention her name.

In fact, although he had never shown any particular interest in Jack, it was clear to everyone, including Jack, that he began to avoid the boy, probably because his dark hair and laughing green eyes reminded him so much of Lady Sarah. It was not many weeks, however, before Jack's eyes were no longer merry. Indeed, although the color of his eyes had remained remarkable, people were more inclined to comment upon their coldness than upon any other quality.

He had been a wild but loving boy until her departure; after that, his wildness increased until his father determined to keep him away from home at all costs. After years of school there had followed the Army and years on the Continent during the war with Napoleon. In fact, only his father's death had called him back to England. He had sold out and come home, not to mourn him but to claim his fortune. For more than a year now he had idled away his time in London, enjoying—as much as he

could enjoy anything—the reputation for reckless-
ness that he had acquired.

Only once since his mother's betrayal had he
given his heart to another woman. He smiled grimly
as he prepared for Landford that evening, suddenly
remembering Olivia, the radiantly beautiful singer
that he had met in Rome. He had mistaken the
brightness of her eyes for affectionate tenderness,
but had been brought to his senses before actually
marrying her when he discovered that those bright
eyes regarded a number of gentlemen with precisely
that same expression and that she, like his mother,
was equally free with her favors.

Olivia had not really had the power to hurt him;
that had been lost long ago, but she had confirmed
his low opinion, not just of the fairer sex, but of
mankind in general. One could expect little of people save amusement. Young Landford was providing
him with that.

Diana, studying him furtively across the table that
night, was keenly aware of his chilly scrutiny—and
of the fact that he seemed more distant than he had
the evening before.

"Perhaps you are regretting inviting me to your
home, sir," she remarked, glancing at him with what
she hoped was a look of cool assessment.

"And why would you think such a thing?" Melville
inquired, lifting an eyebrow. "Have I in some way
failed as a host? Did I not offer you a drink and
inquire whether or not you had dined?"

Diana flushed slightly. "That's not what I mean,
as I am quite certain you realize."

"You give me too much credit, sir," responded

her host lightly. "I assure you that I haven't the least notion what you're referring to. I beg you to enlighten me so that I will not continue to offend you."

Trapped, Diana replied stiffly, "It merely seemed to me that we were able to talk a little more—" She paused, trying to decide precisely what she meant. "A little more freely," she continued. "Last night you appeared interested in what I had to say."

"And I don't now?" he inquired, mildly interested. He had not expected the boy to be so perceptive.

She shook her head thoughtfully. "It's as though—as though you had put up a stone wall, like the one you place around a garden. I feel as though I could reach out and touch it, even though I can't see it."

There was a pause, and Diana forced herself to look up at Melville as coolly as possible. What she had said was perfectly true, and she had felt the difference in his attitude strongly from the moment she had entered his home that evening. By the time they had reached the end of their play the night before, she had known by his amused tone and the warmth in his eye that he had enjoyed her company, and she, curiously enough considering his reputation, had found him almost comfortable to talk to. Now she was less certain of him—and of how to handle herself during the course of the evening. She almost began to fear that Tom could have been in the right of it when he warned her.

Her host met her steady, dark-eyed gaze with interest. "Do you always study those you gamble with so closely?" he inquired.

Diana stared at him, her astonishment genuine. "Well, of course I must study my opponent. How else am I to know how to play against him?"

She noticed with annoyance that his shoulders were shaking slightly, and she was quite certain that he was laughing at her. "I am not, as you doubtless have perceived, sir, as experienced a player as yourself, but I assure you that I am an informed one."

"I have no doubt of that," replied Melville with perfect gravity. "I suspect that, given as many years as I have, you would leave me without a feather to fly with."

She smiled grimly. "That is precisely what I plan to do, sir, despite my lack of years."

He returned her smile, and to her surprise, it appeared to be one of genuine amusement. "Then I must consider myself forewarned," he said, apparently giving himself fully to the game.

To Diana's delight—a carefully concealed delight—her winnings, although modest, were steady. She would have almost suspected him of giving a hand away, but she could see nothing in his manner that indicated such a thing. His chagrin at his every loss and pleasure at his every win seemed sincere, and she could certainly think of no reason for him to wish to lose money to her.

To his surprise, Melville discovered that he was enjoying himself. He watched the boy carefully, knowing that each small addition to the hoard he was gaining was another guinea to be used to save his ladylove. He had mentioned nothing to Landford of Lady Genevieve, and naturally the boy had not mentioned her name either.

What Melville had managed to learn from him was that he had a sincere affection for his sister and his aunt. Although he had not seemed inclined to discuss Cambridge, he had shown no objection to discussing his childhood. When Melville had commiserated with him upon the loss of his parents, Landford had nodded.

"It was difficult," Diana agreed, "but, to be truthful, it is so long ago now that is hard to remember just how I felt. I was fortunate enough to have my sister and Aunt Lavinia, and together we rubbed along quite happily."

"You must miss your sister," Melville observed casually, watching him as he appeared to study his cards. "It is a pity that she is too young for London society."

Diana flushed slightly, but her voice remained calm and she managed a careless shrug. It was not for nothing that she had spent years with Trevor. She could mimic his mannerisms with precision—and often had, even disguising herself as him for a forbidden journey into an assembly at Leamington Spa. There she had danced with the ladies and gambled with the gentlemen, doing each with equal aplomb.

"She will arrive here very soon, so there is no need for me to miss her greatly," she said coolly, placing her cards on the table and lifting her eyes to his. "You are mistaken in thinking she is too young for town." She hoped that the topic would change, for she had no wish to discuss herself in any particular detail.

Without a word, he pushed a stack of guineas toward her, their gold glinting in the candlelight. Now that guineas were no longer minted, their beauty seemed even greater. Somehow one seemed richer when the wealth was measured in guineas.

"I look forward to meeting her upon her arrival," observed Melville unexpectedly, as a footman quietly refilled their glasses. "With your permission, I shall call upon her as soon as she comes to town."

Diana studied her glass, sparkling with claret. She had not thought ahead so far as this, but she was profoundly grateful that no one save Tom knew that she and her aunt had already arrived.

She had told her aunt that she was not feeling quite the thing and had kept indoors during the day and pretended to retire early each evening. Poor Tom had been forced to linger in the shadows, waiting for her to emerge each evening at the appointed time. Diana had kept the footman who had carried her message to Melville in her pay so that she could be readmitted safely to the house each night.

"And why should I not grant my permission?" she asked lightly, lifting the claret to her lips.

It was her host's turn to shrug lightly. "More than one gentleman has warned me away from the ladies in his family," he said, smiling.

"Because of your fatal charm?" inquired Diana, a little tartly. "I suppose the gentlemen in question feared that the ladies might take one glance at you and promptly wish to run away with you?"

Melville glanced at her sharply, surprised by her

reaction, and she forced herself to lean back in the chair with a lazy languor she was far from feeling. Jack Melville was a little too confident for her taste, but she must remember that Trevor would probably find him amusing—except for believing that his sister might be tempted by such a rake.

"I assure you, sir," she drawled, apparently devoting all of her attention to her cards, "I have too complete a confidence in you as a gentleman and my sister as a lady to entertain any doubts about having you meet her."

Melville executed a brief bow, its irony not lost upon Diana. "I am humbly grateful for your good opinion, my lord," he responded.

"In truth," Diana continued, still glued to her cards, "it is my Aunt Lavinia whom I shall have to watch. Although she is advanced in years, she has a very susceptible heart."

Here she glanced up to meet Melville's questioning gaze. "I must ask you, sir, to give me your word that you will not break my aunt's heart."

To her pleasure, his shoulders once again shook slightly, although only a slight light of amusement appeared in his eyes. Once again he bowed.

"I assure you that I shall hold your aunt sacred," he said solemnly.

"I should like to send flowers to your sister to welcome her," he added after a few more minutes of play. "Does she favor daisies as much as you do?" he inquired, indicating the flowers that once again adorned her coat and hat.

Despite the fact that they were playing in a private home rather than under the candle-glare of a gambling hell, Diana had been unwilling to give up her disguise, feeling quite correctly that it provided her some protection.

"That would be most kind of you," Diana observed. "She is very fond of them." And she wondered precisely what Melville had on his mind that he had suddenly become interested in the sister of his gambling partner.

And indeed Melville was asking himself the same question. He had intended to put an end to the play that night, cleaning Landford's pockets and placing Lady Genevieve far beyond his reach. He had, however, found himself even more drawn to the young man than he had been before.

In reaching for a pack of cards, their hands had touched, and Melville had felt a thrill of pleasure that had been a stranger to him for years. He had regarded the young earl uneasily, wondering just what force was at work here, and then he had remembered the sister. If she were anything like Landford, he felt that he might enjoy pursuing the acquaintance—at least for a while. And he decided that he could not cut off the relationship with Landford yet, either. He would not take the young man's money tonight. It would be more amusing to spend a little more time with him.

To Diana's pleasure and Tom's amazement, she won almost £5,000 that evening. He came round early the next morning, before Lady Lavinia had awakened, to discover the outcome of the evening. To his horror, however, Diana informed him that she had every intention of returning to Melville's home that very night.

"You can't do it, Di!" he exclaimed, clutching his hair once more. "You won't win again, you know!"

"And why do you say that, Tom?" she demanded. "If my skills were good enough to win last night, why will they not stand me in good stead again to-night?"

Tom shook his head desperately. "I don't know why he has done it, but Melville has surely let you win!"

Diana looked at him with disfavor. "And just why do you say that?" she again demanded, her tone more ominous.

Even Tom, who was not noted for the quickness of his observations, heard her change in tone. "Don't be angry with me, Di," he pleaded. "Just think about it for a moment. This is a man who is a hardened gamester! He has broken the fortunes of several experienced men and countless young ones that I could name for you. How is it that you won when so many have lost?"

Diana did not reply for a moment, startled by the news that Tom had just imparted. She knew, of course, that Melville was a seasoned player and had won Livingstone House, but she had not realized that he had left such a trail of disasters.

"I'll tell you one thing," he continued, encouraged by her silence. "He has lost to you for a reason."

The silence continued while they stared at one another.

"Perhaps he has heard about Lord Appelby," she said slowly.

Tom shrugged. "That is more than probable. Gossip travels quickly, and that news has made the rounds of the clubs."

"Trevor's affairs are known to everyone?" Diana demanded, incensed by this invasion of her brother's privacy.

Tom patted her arm. "That's the way things are here, Di," he said sympathetically. "It couldn't have remained private. Scandal is the lifeblood of the *ton* and it travels more quickly than you could imagine."

Diana stood up and paced the room restlessly. "Perhaps that explains it. Perhaps that really is why Mr. Melville chose to lose to me," she said suddenly.

Tom stared at her as though she had lost her wits. "What are you talking about, Di?"

When she didn't reply immediately, he asked in disbelief, "You surely don't think that Melville lost to you in order to help you?"

"Well, why should that be so farfetched?" she asked defensively. "He must occasionally feel sympathy for someone."

"Jack Melville?" he said, his eyes wide. "You think that Jack Melville might have lost five thousand pounds to you because he pities Trev?" Here he rubbed his temples, as though he were trying to clear his head. "Di, this is a man who would break another man's fortune in one evening without even blinking! Why would he pity Trevor, whom he doesn't really know, simply because he has a case of what a man like Melville would undoubtedly call calf-love?"

Diana flushed, remembering the unaccountable glimpses of warmth she had seen in Melville. "He is, perhaps, a kinder man than you think, Tom! I am not at all certain that my view is so farfetched as you make it sound."

"Farfetched?" Tom shook his head in disbelief. "Di, it is so very far beyond farfetched that I don't have the words to describe it!"

"Well, you need not search!" she responded tartly. "But I shall need for you to have your mother's carriage waiting for me at the corner at ten o'clock once again tonight."

Tom groaned. "How can you think you will win again? Don't do it, Di! I don't know what deep game he is playing, but you will surely be the loser!"

"Ten o'clock," she replied, walking briskly to the door. "And you must excuse me now, Tom, for I must be back in my bed and ill once more before Aunt Lavinia comes down for breakfast."

Six

The day passed slowly for Diana, who paced her room restlessly except when Lady Lavinia came to check on her, and even more slowly for the nervous Tom, who had to spend most of it with Trevor, trying to keep him from gambling and trying not to think about the approaching evening.

Finally, exhausted by his efforts to divert Trevor from a game of backgammon at Brooks's, where the stakes were high, he suggested in desperation that they call upon Diana and Lady Lavinia. He knew well enough that Diana would call him to account for that later, since she had no desire to explain her convenient illness to Trevor. She had put him off yesterday afternoon by sending a note to him, saying that they would be with the dressmaker all afternoon and that she expected both she and their aunt to be exhausted afterwards.

When they reached Lady Lavinia's home, Trevor was shocked to learn of Diana's indisposition.

"Ill?" he responded in disbelief when his aunt had explained the circumstances to him. "That's impossible, Aunt! You know that Di is never ill! Why, I spoke to her just this morning!"

"I think perhaps she has been putting a good face

upon things for you. She has the headache and I think the trip has been too much for her—" Lavinia began, but her nephew cut her off.

"She would never be thrown off her stride by such a thing," he protested, growing more alarmed by the minute. "She thrives on change. You know that there's nothing missish about Di."

He stared at his aunt for a moment while Tom nervously fingered the arm of the sofa. After apparently thinking things over, Trevor turned toward the door, announcing, "I'm just going to bob up and have a look at her, Aunt. I want to feel certain in my own mind that it's nothing more serious than a headache."

Fortunately Diana heard her brother's approach and had time to prostrate herself upon the bed, pressing a handkerchief soaked in sal volatile to her forehead. Trevor's nose wrinkled in distaste as he entered the room, and he opened the window wider.

"Good Lord, Di! You'll choke to death if you breathe in too much of that dratted stuff!" he exclaimed, turning to scrutinize her. "What's all this about your being out of sorts? This isn't like you at all. You seemed perfectly all right yesterday morning and this morning."

Diana opened her eyes only partially, as though the light hurt her, and managed a weak smile. "I feel at my best early in the mornings. I daresay I shall feel more the thing after another night's good rest," she murmured, pressing the handkerchief more firmly to her forehead and partially concealing her face with her hand. She knew that she did not look as sickly as she should, but she hoped to divert his attention to other matters.

"How does Jenny go on?" she asked, trying to make her voice as faint as possible.

"She is most unhappy, needless to say," her brother replied, momentarily distracted from the matter at hand. "Tom and I went to the theater last night because he had learned that she intended to be there. I remembered what you said about taking care of Tom, and so I allowed myself to be gulled instead of going off to the Cocoa Tree or Brooks's."

"And did you see her there?" inquired Diana.

Trevor, pacing the room, shook his head. "Of course we did not! I was certain that Tom was trying to keep me from gambling, just as you had told me. I didn't want to be responsible for any further lunatic behavior, so I went along with him."

"How good a friend you are, Trev!" she murmured. And it was true. Knowing how desperately he wanted to win the money for Jenny, it must have taken considerable sacrifice—more than he was usually willing to make—in order to go along with Tom. "What did he say when Jenny did not come?" she asked curiously, wondering about Tom's ability to improvise.

"He said that her mother must have changed her mind at the last moment, but we stayed even through the pantomime, for he insisted that they might come in late. He acted quite downcast for having misled me, but then we went to her home and sat discreetly just down the street, hoping to catch a glimpse of her when she returned from her evening out. I wanted to be certain that she had not been forced to be in company with Treffington."

He sighed. "We must have sat there for an hour, but it began to drizzle and Tom insisted that we go home since I had felt unwell the evening before." The mention of his own illness recalled him to the matter at hand.

"And why did not you or our aunt let me know that you were ill, Di?" he asked, fixing his gaze upon her as sternly as he could manage.

"There was no point in oversetting you when you already have so much to contend with," replied his sister, closing her eyes as though in pain.

Alarmed by her unusual behavior, he changed tactics immediately and patted her hand. "I'm sorry, Di," he said remorsefully. "I'm the greatest beast in nature to keep at you when you're not feeling well. I'll send Aunt up immediately."

Diana opened her eyes as the door closed gently behind him. It was too bad to deceive him in such a way, she thought regretfully, but it was for his own good. He would forgive her when he knew what she was doing.

For a moment she tried to picture his expression when he learned that she had been gambling with Melville in private, then hastily dismissed that line of thought as unprofitable. There was no need to get up in the boughs over Trevor; she had too much to do. She put all thought of her brother firmly from her mind and concentrated on the evening to come.

When she entered Melville's library that evening, she was at once aware that there was something different in the atmosphere. She had always, even as a child, been keenly sensitive to the emotional state of other people, knowing immediately when she entered a room whether or not the people were distressed. She did not have to hear their tone of voice, merely the expression in their eyes and the manner in which they held themselves were enough.

Melville, she saw at once, was on edge. She had known the evening before that he had attempted to place an emotional barrier between them—why she couldn't imagine, since there was more enjoyment for both of them when there was no such barrier. She had watched it lower last night until he seemed quite natural, his wicked humor showing again and his pleasure in her replies evident.

Tonight he seemed to have withdrawn once more, and she could only speculate upon the reason, deciding that she would watch tonight, rather than blurting out her thoughts as she had yesterday evening. He seemed a curious sort of man. He was not, she thought, as wicked as he would have others— perhaps even himself—believe. She had caught glimpses of warmth in their conversation that did not fit with the picture of himself he presented to the world. He was, she thought, a very interesting— and very attractive—individual.

Although Diana was not considered "out" as yet, not having been officially presented, she had always moved in adult society because of her aunt's friends. She had never been a schoolroom miss and her contact with men had never been limited to the company of her brother and uncle. That was, in fact, one of the many things that her uncle considered regrettable about her upbringing, feeling that it had made her far too self-assured and outspoken for a woman.

As they settled down to play, she watched Melville carefully, and was—as she had at first been the night before—chilled when she encountered his gaze. After half an hour of silent play, she had better reason still to feel chilled. She had lost £500.

She leaned back in her chair with what she hoped was easy nonchalance and stretched out her doe-skin-clad legs to inspect her shining boots. "You appear to be having quite a streak of luck, Melville," she said casually.

"You could call it that," he returned briefly, shuffling the cards with the ease born of long practice.

Nettled, Diana took his reply to mean that skill, rather than luck, had caused him to win. While she herself believed that skillful play was more important than luck—and had often pointed that out to Trevor—she found the observation less acceptable when applied to herself.

"Well, we shall see if your luck holds, sir," she replied briskly, studying her cards with grim determination.

Despite himself, Melville watched his guest with rising amusement. Landford's thoughts seemed crystal clear to him, and the boy's attempts to pass off his loss as inconsequential were almost pitiable. Still, he reminded himself, Landford would be better off learning the truth about love—and about himself—now rather than later. Just as he was certain that the boy's friendship with Ralston would disappoint and that the affair with Appelby's daughter would be disillusioning if it were allowed to continue, he was equally certain that the boy himself would be guilty of betrayal if given a strong enough motive—like desire. It was, he thought, more than time for the boy to become better acquainted with his own weaknesses and with the ways of the world. He was, Melville assured himself, giving the boy a lesson in life which would help him to survive, although assuredly he would not thank his teacher for it. Perhaps he would offer the boy a choice.

"Indeed we shall," he said pleasantly, "but before we continue, why not take a moment for supper? I did not dine earlier, and I find myself ravenous."

Suspicious of this sudden change in manner, Diana eyed him for a moment, then nodded, placing her cards face-down on the table.

"They are quite safe, I assure you," said her host. "We shall not be three steps away, and you may keep your eyes upon them at all times. Burbage will serve us here by the fire."

Here he indicated two chairs set at a comfortable distance from the hearth, a butler's tray between them. Diana joined him somewhat reluctantly. She wished to continue playing rather than place herself in a situation where she would be under still closer scrutiny than she had been already. Too, she did not wish to drink any of the champagne that Burbage was serving with the scalloped oysters, not only because she wished a very clear head for play, but also because gentlemen had the unfortunate habit of keeping chamber pots in a nearby cupboard so that they could relieve themselves without the inconvenience of leaving the room. Even with the relative privacy provided by a screen, for her, of course, there could be no such relief; so she sipped her drink carefully, inspecting the room longingly for a plant where she might be able to rid herself of it.

Melville watched her closely, certain that Landford wished a clear head for the game and suspecting that he wished to dispose of the drink. When the boy's gaze suddenly rested upon a potted palm in a far corner of the room next to a curtained alcove, his eyes lit up.

"I see that you are admiring my palm tree," Melville said smoothly. "It is from Egypt, and I usually keep it in the conservatory, which offers it a better climate than does this room."

Diana looked at him sharply, half afraid that he had indeed read her mind. Doing her best to conceal her reaction, she rose and strolled over to it, giving her best imitation of her brother's long-limbed, casual gait.

"It's a pretty thing," she said carelessly, reaching out to touch one of the leaves.

Melville, joining her, nodded. Glancing at the glass she held in her hand, he added, "It is not particularly fond of champagne, however. A friend of mine tried watering it from a magnum of the stuff, and the poor thing almost died. The gardener would never have forgiven me."

Diana, aware of his amusement, felt her irritation mounting. "Your plant is quite safe from me," she assured him, her face and her voice stiff. She would have to be more careful. She had already known that Melville was a very intelligent man, and he appeared to be far more perceptive than she had given him credit for.

"I daresay your sister is very fond of plants," Melville said absently, quite as though he were thinking about something else altogether.

Diana glanced at him sharply once more, but he appeared to be studying the palm with peculiar intensity. "My sister? Yes, I suppose she is. Why do you ask, sir?"

"Just an idle thought," replied Melville, draining his glass. "I thought you might have learned your affection for flowers from her, since you seem to be quite fond of them yourself. I have noticed that your hat is always wreathed with yellow roses or daisies—very attractively arranged, I might add."

"My valet looks after me well," said Diana nonchalantly. "Since it is the fashion of the day, he does not wish me to appear at a gambling table with an unadorned hat. I would not be a credit to him then, so he is quite firm about it."

"Then I fear that I must put Burbage sadly out of countenance," returned her host, who had yet to appear in the frieze coat and gaily bedecked hat affected by many gentlemen of the *ton*. He was dressed simply but elegantly in a well-cut dark jacket and breeches.

Flushing, Diana hastened to amend her slip. "I assure you, sir, that I intended no criticism of your own dress—which is, of course, impeccable."

"You relieve me," Melville said gravely. "I will tell Burbage that he has no reason to hang his head."

"You needn't mock me, sir," said Diana, her color mounting even more. "You know full well that I intended no insult."

"And none was taken," he assured her affably. "I

had merely wondered, however, if your love of flowers was learned from your aunt—or, perhaps, as I mentioned, from your sister. However, it is of no importance."

Melville was annoyed with himself for feeling any interest at all in the absent sister. More troubling still was his continued interest in the boy.

"You may soon ask her yourself about her interest in flowers," she replied, studying her cards as they once again seated themselves at the table. "She and my aunt have arrived for their visit, and as I recall, last night you indicated a desire to meet them." She found herself wondering just how it would be to meet him when she was Diana once more instead of Trevor.

"Indeed I did," responded her host, sounding almost bored with the subject now, although she was aware that he was watching her carefully without appearing to do so.

Diana nodded without speaking, trying to appear absorbed in her play while wondering about his questions.

In a few moments she had no need to pretend, for she once again lost to Melville and now found herself £1,000 in the hole.

"Shall we call it an evening?" inquired Melville, deciding almost against his will to give the boy a chance to escape. He was certain that Landford would refuse, and he was correct.

Diana shook her head stiffly. She felt a knot forming in her stomach, but she was determined. After all, she still had money at her disposal, and she was reasonably confident that she could manage to win the next hand. Melville was, however, a much more astute player than she had given him credit for being. She found herself hoping desperately that Burbage would keep his master's glass full and that Melville would begin to show some sign of having drunk too much.

"I shall soon come about, sir," she replied firmly. "I always do."

"Do you?" he responded. "That is fortunate, indeed. I should hate for you to feel a false confidence, however."

"What do you mean by that?" she demanded, very much upon her guard.

He leaned back in his chair and smiled what Tom would have immediately termed his "croc smile." "Why, merely that I always come about myself. It will be difficult for us both to do so."

"Then I shall be sorry for you," said Diana carelessly, attempting to achieve a manner as casual as his own.

Melville inclined his head briefly at this kindly remark and signaled to Burbage to refill their glasses. Diana groaned inwardly, resolving to dispose of hers in the fire if her host would but disappear behind the screen for a few moments. To be found again beside the palm tree would undoubtedly excite his suspicions, but he could not be surprised if she were warming herself by the fire.

Unfortunately, however, Melville showed no sign of taking the desired journey, and their play continued unabated for the next two hours. At the end of that time, Diana was horrified to realize that she owed him all the money she had won from him the evening before.

"It is growing late," observed her host. "Shall we say double or nothing on the next hand?"

Almost without thinking, Diana nodded. She had to do this. She stared at her cards with terrible intensity. If she were not to fail Trevor, she had to be successful.

And, somewhat to her surprise, she was. Only a few minutes later, she was the proud possessor of £10,000. One-tenth of what Trevor needs, she thought in satisfaction, once again leaning back in her chair and trying not to heave a sigh of relief. She had every intention of calling it an evening and taking her winnings home.

Melville, however, had other plans. He had his victim precisely where he wished him, and he planned to reel him in.

"I see that you were quite right, Landford," he remarked. "You do seem to come about."

Diana nodded briefly, studying the toe of her boot and waiting for the moment when she could announce that she must be leaving.

"Perhaps you could give me the opportunity to recover my loss in a way that will not take any of your cash. Let us make the evening more interesting," Melville drawled.

Diana looked at him sharply, wondering just what he had to propose. Melville appeared to be gazing absently at the candles flickering in the chandelier, but she did not believe for a moment that his mind was less than razor-sharp—nor that he did not have in mind a definite agenda.

"And what would that be?" she inquired. "I must trust that it would not take long, for I am beginning to feel quite weary."

"As I am myself," he responded. "No, my proposition will not take long at all. It is merely this." Here he paused, and Diana forced herself to lean back comfortably in her chair, quite as though what he would say had no particular importance for her.

"I must confess, Landford, that I have discovered a little more about you than you might wish me to know," he continued, transferring his gaze from the candles to the face of the young man opposite him.

Immediately on her guard, Diana held herself firmly in check and responded with admirable coolness. "And what is it that you have discovered, Mr. Melville?" she inquired.

"I have learned that you wish to marry and that certain obstacles have been placed in your path. That is an unfortunate situation for a young man in love."

"Yes, it certainly is," said Diana grimly. "May I ask just how you came by this information, sir?"

"I fear that your unfortunate love affair has become food for gossip in the clubs now," said Melville. "All the world—at least all of our little world—is aware that Lord Appelby requested a most unreasonable amount of you in return for the hand of his daughter."

He saw with admiration that Landford betrayed no emotion other than a slight flickering of his lashes; his gaze remained steadily upon Melville. Diana nodded slightly and he continued, "It has come to me, Landford, that I might be able to help you."

At this unexpected remark, Diana, who had been preparing herself for something quite different, momentarily forgot herself. "And how could you possibly help me, sir?" she demanded, leaning toward him eagerly.

"I am no philanthrophist," Melville countered, somewhat amused by the boy's unaffected response. He had known that Landford would take the bait. "What I propose would also provide a reward for me, should I win."

When he paused, Diana prodded him. "Do continue, Mr. Melville. Just what is your proposition?" she inquired anxiously. It would be a stroke of unbelievable good fortune if she could return home to tell Trevor that he would be able to marry Jenny.

"Simply this. If you win the next hand, I will pay the remaining ninety thousand pounds you need for Appelby."

"And if I lose?" she asked, her mouth suddenly dry. Even the mention of so much money made her slightly ill, and she feared that he would be asking something she could not grant.

"If you lose, then I will give you a choice: I will either call it even and say that you owe me no money at all, or I will pay you the money you need for Appelby, if—"

"If what?" prompted Diana eagerly.

"If you will give me your sister's hand in marriage," responded Melville smoothly. "How can you lose?"

There was a barely perceptible pause while her mind raced. What on earth could he be playing at? He would lose money in any case, win or lose. Why, she wondered, would he offer her such a choice? Her eyebrows arched slightly as she considered the matter. Even if she lost, she would win. And, if she were willing to say that she would marry him, Trevor would have Jenny.

"What do you say, sir?" drawled Melville, studying his victim closely without appearing to do so. He could almost hear the boy's thoughts as he considered the choices. It was possible, of course, that Landford would refuse the offer of marriage, for he had carefully offered an escape. The boy could lose and still walk away from the debt and leave all of this behind him. From what Melville had seen of human nature, however, he was quite sure that the boy would sacrifice his sister, no matter how deep his affection for her, for the sake of the young woman that he wanted for himself.

"I accept your offer, Mr. Melville," said Diana calmly, settling herself for the decisive game. She had no notion what he was playing at, but his offer was their golden opportunity. Win or lose, Trevor would be able to marry Jenny, and even if she lost, she would be able to think herself out of the problem of marrying Mr. Melville.

She glanced across the table at him, self-possessed and now laughing-eyed. Of course, she thought, shocking herself, even if the marriage to him were a necessary part of the wager, she might find the wedding interesting—more interesting than she had once thought possible.

Seven

Tom stared at her, bewildered. He had hurried over as soon as he decently could the next morning, anxious to know how she had fared with Melville. Her response, however, had been anything but clear, and he began to wonder if he were hearing her properly.

"Sit down, Tom," she said patiently, her cheeks glowing. "It's good news, you know. Trevor will be able to marry Jenny now."

"But Di, you said that you had won—and that you had lost. How could you do both?" he asked slowly, speaking as precisely as he could. He was beginning to feel that they were speaking two different languages.

"It's really very simple," Diana replied, reflecting privately that it was anything but simple to understand. "I made a wager with Melville and I lost."

"You lost, and so naturally you have a hundred thousand pounds to give to Trev." He shook his head. "I think it's you that had better sit down, Diana," he responded. "You're all about in your head. I'll ring for the butler to have Lady Lavinia come down, and she'll take care of you. I think you are simply overtired. The strain of the past few days has been too much for you and you are truly ill now."

"Nonsense, Tom," she laughed, taking his arm and pulling him down onto the sofa beside her. "There's nothing wrong with me, and Aunt Lavinia will know what has happened soon enough. The least I can do is to allow her her rest."

"Well, I wish—at least I think that I wish—that you would tell me what happened, Di. I haven't yet made heads nor tails of what you're saying," he complained, rubbing his temples in anticipation of a headache.

In fact, he had felt for the past several days as though he were suffering from a sort of ongoing headache, and he had hoped from morning to morning to be rid of it at last. He looked at her hopefully, thinking that she might be about to free him of his problems.

And it must be admitted that Diana looked remarkably bright-eyed for one who had sat up so late and arisen so early. Nor did she look at all downcast, as could well be expected of someone who had lost a wager of the magnitude that she had indicated. Tom prepared himself to be cheered. Perhaps he had simply misunderstood.

"Come now, Di, we're sitting down, so I am prepared for your news. Do tell me as plainly as you can," he urged her.

"Well, you needn't look so grim," she laughed. "One would think that you were prepared to hear the bleakest of news."

Determined to get to the bottom of the matter, no matter how painful the outcome, Tom persevered. "I understood you to say that you lost your final wager last night, Di, and you said that had you won, you would have had enough for Trev to pay Appelby."

She nodded. "Yes, that's quite true."

Tom's eyes had grown large and he was forced to clear his throat before he could continue. "But you lost?" he whispered, watching her with painful intensity.

Diana nodded gaily. "Yes, I did, Tom, but you needn't look so panic-stricken. I didn't lose a hundred thousand pounds. Melville agreed to pay that amount as part of the wager—even if I lost."

Despite this cheerful news, Tom's chest felt as though metal bands laced about it were being tightened. "You lost, and yet Melville is still paying you that sum?"

Again she nodded encouragingly, thinking that she had never seen Tom looking quite so peculiar. "Do you need a glass of brandy, Tom?" she inquired anxiously. "Should I ring for—"

He shook his head vehemently and managed to croak, "What did you lose, Di?"

"Myself," she replied simply. "Melville said that if I lost the hand, he would still pay me the money, but that he would gain my sister's hand in marriage—which means mine, of course."

Tom's eyes almost started from his head as he collapsed against the back of the sofa. Concerned, she rose and started toward the bell pull to ring for help, but he feebly waved her away from it.

"You can't marry that man," he whispered.

She laughed. "Well, naturally I shan't marry

him," she agreed. "Or at least I would, of course, if he wished me to since I made the wager, but I don't believe he has the least desire to marry anyone—least of all someone he has never met. Or at least someone he doesn't think he has met."

Tom stared at her as at one possessed. "What are you talking about, Di?" he demanded. "Did you promise that you would marry him or did you not?"

"I promised him my sister's hand in marriage," she explained patiently. "But naturally I have no sister, and I think he did it as some kind of test for me—or actually for Trevor. When push comes to shove, he won't wish to go through with it."

"But you pledged Trev's word that Melville could marry you?" Tom asked in disbelief.

She smiled again, but a little less certainly this time. "Yes, that's what I've just been telling you, Tom."

"Then you have pledged yourself to marry him," Tom stated flatly, asking her no question this time. "And what will you do, Diana, if he decides to go through with it?"

She paused a moment, then sat down beside him. Until this moment, she had been perfectly certain that Melville had not the slightest intention of leg-shackling himself for life. But what if he had indeed decided to do so and had decided that anyone would do—even a woman won in a game of cards? Attractive though she found him, the sudden thought that he might have decided anyone would do as a marital partner, even a girl won in a card game, was most unwelcome. He had certainly indicated that he had no use for love, so this would be a business arrangement entirely, and Diana the price of the bargain.

"And, Di," Tom added, seeing that he had her attention now and playing his ace, "what are we to tell Trev?"

At that most inopportune of moments, the drawing room door flew open and the gentleman in question strolled into the chamber.

"Well, you're looking better this morning, Di," he commented, scrutinizing her as he sat down easily, "but you look a wreck, Tom. What's happened to put you up in the boughs?"

Tom and Diana looked at one another for a moment, then she said simply, "We've something to tell you, Trev."

When she had finished her explanation, her brother sat staring at her blankly, wearing the same expression that had appeared the moment she told him that she had returned to the Chateau Royale and played with Melville, still attired as Lord Landford. His frozen features had caused Tom to hurry over to a decanter of brandy and pour his friend a stiff drink. When he tried to press it into Trevor's hand, however, it was simply brushed aside, so Tom sat down and disposed of it himself, wishing earnestly that he were miles away from London and deciding that his liver was in need of some fresh country air.

When he was finally capable of motion, Trevor leaped to his feet and paced the room, running his hands through his hair as though he would like to tear it out in clumps.

"I'll call him out! By heaven, how dare he say

such a thing to my sister!" he demanded furiously. "How could he have the gall to think that he could win you in a game of cards as though you were a horse or a diamond bracelet! I'll see him at the end of a dueling pistol before the day is out!"

Tom closed his eyes briefly, seeing his friend lying dead on some dew-covered field at dawn while he stood there helplessly, his loyal, and totally inexperienced second, and Melville carelessly tossed his own pistol to the ground and strode to his carriage, departing no doubt for a hearty breakfast without a thought for the carnage he had left behind him. Tom moaned softly.

"And I'd like to know what you have to sigh about, Tom Ralston!" Trevor added, turning on his friend. "You're the one that aided and abetted her! She has destroyed her reputation and mine with her behavior! What were you thinking of to allow her to put herself into the hands of such a man?"

"Tom did his best to stop me," Diana said, stepping quickly between them, "but you know very well that he could not have done so, Trev. And when he knew that he could not, he did his best to watch over me."

Trevor snorted, but before he could begin his tirade again, she added, "And if you truly care about our reputations, Trev, you won't call Melville out. If you do, all of the *ton* will discover what we might otherwise be able to keep secret."

"She's right, you know," said Tom suddenly, the sense of what she was saying dawning upon him. "As it is, no one knows about her charade, not even Melville himself. But if you fight a duel, it will never be kept a secret—and very likely you'll either be killed or have to flee the country."

"You're a great help, Tom," remarked his friend bitterly, falling into a chair and staring at Tom and Diana as though he had never seen them before. A long pause ensued before he reluctantly added, "But I can see that you're right."

Before either of them could say anything, he continued, "I may not be able to fight a duel with him, but by all that's holy, I'll call him to a personal accounting! He needn't think that he can treat us like this and get away with it scot-free!"

Tom, who had been reflecting that anyone who married Diana would scarcely be getting away scot-free, said hesitantly, "But won't that be almost as bad, Trev? If you do that, you'll still be stirring up a dust, and right now he doesn't even know that he hasn't been playing cards with you."

"Tom's right," added Diana swiftly, before Trevor could attack him. She knew his quick flares of temper well, and she knew that the worst was over. "Just think about it, Trevor. You will have the money to keep Jenny from having to marry Treffington. Neither Melville nor anyone else will know that you were not the one who played cards with him—and I doubt seriously that he has any real intention of marrying me, but we can deal with that if and when it comes."

Trevor sat for several minutes in silence, the two of them watching him as he nervously drummed his fingers on the arm of the chair.

"Whatever possessed you, Di?" he demanded finally. "Of course you will do no such thing as marry him, but in the meantime, think of how this makes me look! Melville—and everyone else in the *ton*—will believe that I would gamble away my sister for my own happiness!"

"But no one except Melville will know, my dear," she insisted. "Or they won't unless we botch things ourselves. And what can it matter what he thinks? After all, he is the one who came up with the idea."

Trevor shook his head. "You don't understand, Di. I must straighten this out, or I won't be able to look at myself in the mirror."

She pulled her chair close to his and took his hand. "If you are truly concerned about me and my reputation, Trevor, you will let this matter lie. As I said, the chances are that he has no intention of marrying me. Do be sensible, my dear," she added, stroking his hair. "Just think of Jenny and what this will mean to the two of you. You can't have her marrying Treffington."

"By Jupiter, no!" agreed Tom, shuddering.

"Do you really think we might come out of this all right?" asked Trevor, willing at last to listen.

"Of course," Diana responded confidently. "You will save Jenny, and all will be well."

Tom, seeing that his friend was growing rapidly more mellow, again pressed a glass of brandy into his hand. He wanted very much to believe Diana's assurances himself, but recent bitter experience had taught him that her idea of all being well did not necessarily coincide with his own. He hoped that the brandy might keep Trevor from suffering the same misgiving.

After swallowing the brandy in one fiery gulp,

Trevor turned to the other two. "What do you think we should do now?" he asked.

Diana hugged him. "I knew that you would see that this is the answer, Trevor. The first thing that you should do is to invite Melville here to meet me, just as though doing so were the most natural thing in the world. He will be expecting it. And the second thing is to see Lord Appelby and arrange for the money."

Her brother's face had darkened at the mention of Melville, but the change in expression when the money was mentioned was almost ludicrous.

"On second thought, I think that you had best settle things with Lord Appelby immediately," she said, recognizing the weakness and determined to keep him on the proper course. "There is no saying that he might not decide to give way to Treffington earlier than he had promised if his creditors are too pressing."

"That's true," added Tom, following her lead. "I heard only yesterday that he has lost his carriage and those splendid bays to Albertson. At this rate, he'll soon be forced to walk everywhere."

"Well, Jenny shall not have to live in such a manner," announced Trevor firmly, "and certainly she shall not be sacrificed for her father's debts. I intend to remove her from that household as soon as possible."

Leaving Diana and Tom to take care of arranging the financial matters, he departed for a meeting with Appelby, determined to wrest from him approval for his marriage to Jenny upon the presentation of the money that night.

Tom eyed her dubiously after he had left. "Well, Di, what are you going to do about Melville?" he inquired.

"Why, I shall see him, of course," she responded lightly, sounding more self-confident than she felt. "He will send the money over by one of his men, but I am certain that he will be calling very soon."

For the moment she hesitated, remembering the change in his attitude last night. It was true that he had at first expressed a strong interest in meeting her, planning to call immediately when she came to town, but last night he had seemed almost blasé about the idea, despite his bet. Still, she felt quite certain that he was playing some sort of game for his own amusement, and that, she thought, would require his coming to see how matters were progressing.

"Once I see him," she continued, straightening her shoulders as she thought of it, "I shall know what his attitude toward the engagement is, and I shall be greatly surprised if he wishes to become legshackled to me—or to anyone." She would not allow herself to dwell upon the thought that he might be purchasing her as he would any other commodity deemed necessary for his life.

Tom, who could not think of anything that would horrify him more than the prospect of becoming engaged to Diana and living in constant fear of what she might do next, was nevertheless not certain that Melville would dismiss her so lightly.

"Perhaps you are too certain," he said hesitantly, giving voice to her nagging fear. "After all, Di, why should he *not* wish to marry you? Perhaps he has decided that it is time for him to take a wife, and you would certainly be an eligible choice—even if a civilized man wouldn't go about it in this manner."

"It isn't my impression that he is the marrying kind," she said, realizing with sudden discomfort that this was indeed her impression. And the realization should have made her feel better instead of leaving her with an empty feeling in the pit of her stomach."

"Hello, my dears," said Aunt Lavinia brightly, entering the room with her usual light step. "I'm so glad to see that you're feeling better, Diana," she added warmly.

She settled comfortably on the sofa and smiled at them both. "I have felt so out of touch for the past few days. Do tell me what has been happening, Tom."

Diana and Tom glanced at each other, and Tom cleared his throat nervously as he rose. "I am most awfully sorry, Lady Lavinia, but I think that I should be going now," he murmured, pulling out his pocketwatch and regarding it earnestly. I am to see my tailor at two."

"Sit back down, Tom," said Diana, catching his eye and holding it. "You will have more than enough time to get to your appointment."

Here she turned toward Lady Lavinia. "Dear Aunt," she began, "we have so much to tell you that it's difficult for me to know just where to begin."

Tom gave one last, longing look at the door that led to freedom, sank down onto his chair, and proceeded to give his full and studious attention to a painting on the opposite wall.

Eight

Unfortunately, not seeing Lady Lavinia's face did not protect him from hearing her, from the first horrified gasp to the "Oh, no, Diana, you did *not!*"'s that punctuated Diana's story to the protracted silence at the end that finally drove Tom to glance at her surreptitiously. Her normally pink cheeks were pale and she was leaning back among the cushions of the sofa, eyes closed, her expression as tragic as her deep dimples would allow. Diana was waving a vinaigrette under her nose, and Tom hurried once again to the brandy decanter, hoping that their news had not been responsible for an attack of any sort. His own liver was aching in furious sympathy as he pressed the glass to her lips.

"Just a sip, Lady Lavinia," he murmured encouragingly. "See if this won't make you feel more the thing."

She sat up abruptly and pushed the glass away, choking slightly. "No, thank you, Tom," she said weakly. "Spirits make me violently ill."

Having done the only thing he could think of, he sat down close to her, relieved to see that some of the color was returning to her cheeks.

"How could you have done such a perfectly scandalous thing!" she demanded, regaining her voice.

"Well, ma'am, I'm afraid that I can make no excuse—" Tom began, his eyes returning to the portrait.

"No, Tom, I don't mean you!" she intervened. "I know Diana and I am certain you couldn't help yourself. It is you I am addressing, my dear," Lavinia said, turning to her niece. "How can we possibly avert a scandal? It will ruin all of you, child!"

"You needn't fear a scandal, Aunt," returned Diana calmly. "There will not be one."

At her words, Lavinia's eyebrows rose almost as high as those of Tom. "Not be one? How can it possibly be escaped?" she demanded.

"Well, just think of it, Aunt. Who is going to tell anyone about it? Will you do so?"

Lavinia gasped, her plump cheeks quivering with indignation. "I should think not!"

"Of course not," said Diana, patting her arm consolingly. "Nor will I, nor Tom, nor Trevor, nor Jenny—nor Lord Appelby, who merely wants his money and would not do anything to endanger it."

"What of this man Melville?" Lavinia asked faintly. "Why would he not make the matter known? He scarcely seems a gentleman."

"Whether he is or not has little bearing on the situation. If he decides to marry me—no, Aunt, that is not going to happen, so sit up and attend to what I am saying." Diana interrupted her explanation as Lavinia fell back against the cushions once more, one hand searching for her vinaigrette.

"If he decides to marry me," she continued, "he

will scarcely bandy it abroad that he won me in a card game. Even he has more pride than that."

"And if either of you decides there is to be no marriage, what's to keep him from telling the story to every gossipmonger in the *ton*?" asked Tom, unable to stop himself.

"Who would believe him?" Diana asked simply. "There is nothing in writing, and since Trevor obviously won a good bit of money from him in order to be able to pay Lord Appelby's debts, Melville would merely appear to be a poor loser. And I am certain that he has more pride than to allow such a rumor to begin."

Tom stared at her, his jaw dropping slightly, as he carefully reviewed her point. "Do you know, Lady Lavinia," he said, taking that lady's hand in his own and squeezing it. "I believe that she may be in the right of it!"

Becoming more cheerful with each passing moment, Tom bade the two of them good morning and took himself home to prepare for his call upon his tailor. After he had left, the two ladies sat together quietly, Lavinia reviving herself with a cup of strong tea and Diana gathering her strength for the interview with Melville that she had no doubt was soon approaching.

"Mr. Barton!" exclaimed Lavinia suddenly, setting down her china cup with a sharp click as the color once more drained from her face. "Diana, whatever shall we do about Mr. Barton?"

Diana dismissed him with a careless wave of her hand. "We will contend with him when we must, Aunt. If we take one problem at a time, you know that we will be able to work it out when the time comes."

Her bracing tone was lost on Lady Lavinia. Her aunt did not appear to feel that she knew any such thing, for she rose from the sofa a little shakily, saying, "I believe I'll just go up to my chamber and lie down, my dear. A short nap should do wonders for my spirits."

If she felt it unlikely that she would be able to sleep or that if she did the spectre of Robert Barton might haunt her slumber, she at least did not say so, but Diana watched her leave with a deep feeling of guilt. She knew how much her aunt dreaded confrontations of any sort, particularly those with Uncle Robert, which were always particularly unpleasant, for he was unfailingly critical both of Trevor and Diana and the manner in which their aunt had reared them.

She resolutely dismissed the problem from her mind, however. She firmly believed what she had told Lavinia: if she focused on one problem at a time, she would be able to take care of matters—even Uncle Robert.

She had just risen from the sofa when Tibbett stepped into the room and announced, "Mr. Jack Melville, my lady."

"Please show him in, Tibbett," she said calmly—far more calmly than she felt. Although she had said that she expected him to come, she had not been certain that he would appear today, and she was even less certain of what his attitude would be and what her appropriate response should be. To her annoyance, he strode into the room before she could completely think things through.

As Melville entered the room, he glanced about it quickly before bowing to her. "Forgive me for intruding upon you when you are alone, ma'am. I am a—" He paused for a moment over the word. "I am a companion of your brother's. Perhaps you would prefer that I return when he is here to introduce us properly?"

Diana smiled and extended her hand. "Not at all, Mr. Melville. My brother has spoken of you, and I am happy to make your acquaintance."

Seating himself with an easy attitude that somewhat annoyed her, he smiled. "I understand that you are a lover of flowers, Lady Diana. I have taken the liberty of bringing you a bouquet of daisies and yellow roses. Your butler is taking care of them for you."

"How very kind of you, Mr. Melville. I am indeed fond of flowers—particularly of those you have mentioned. I see that my brother has been boring you with gossip about his family. I must apologize for him."

"I wasn't bored at all, I assure you—quite the contrary. I have found your brother very interesting."

Here he fixed his gaze upon her in a most unsettling manner, studying her intently. "I had not heard, my lady, that you and your brother favored one another so strongly." And indeed he had been taken aback when he had first seen her. Here were the same eyes and hair, the same striking coloring.

"I have been told that we resemble one another strongly," Diana admitted. "We are twins, of course, but as you know very often a brother and sister who are twins look little enough alike."

"Well, that is certainly not the case with you and Landford," replied Melville, his green eyes searching hers as he continued softly. "I should like very much to see the two of you side by side, but I must confess, my lady, that I am pleased that he is not here this morning."

"Indeed?" she inquired politely, lifting an eyebrow and waiting, making a conscious effort to look as distant as possible.

He nodded, taking out a snuff box and flipping it open smoothly with one finger. "It is much better that we are alone. It will give us an opportunity to become acquainted—and it is essential that we do so."

Diana lifted an eyebrow. "I by no means know all of my brother's friends, so I cannot see that our becoming acquainted is at all essential, Mr. Melville," she replied coolly, trying to act as calm as possible even though her heart had suddenly begun to beat wildly. What on earth did the man think he was doing?

There was a silence while he regarded her thoughtfully. "It may well be that you are correct, Lady Diana. The best marriages may indeed be those in which the parties are not acquainted with one another. I admit that I had not expected such a cynical view in one so young, however."

"I am afraid, sir, that you are amusing yourself at my expense," she said, rising. "I do not pretend to understand what you are saying, so if you will forgive me—"

"It really is quite simple, my lady. You and I are to be married," he returned blandly, failing to rise as she did.

Diana moved toward the door, avoiding his eye. "I think that it would be best if you spoke with my brother, Mr. Melville. I shall tell him that you called."

"Oh, I have already spoken with Landford," he responded, still not standing up as a gentleman should when a lady has risen. "He is well aware that we are to be married. You see, I won you from him in a card game last night."

Diana did not have to pretend to be outraged when she turned to face him. The man had boundless audacity and an absolute absence of breeding! If she had not known beforehand about the engagement, such an announcement would have been infuriating and devastating. As matters stood, it was simply infuriating.

"I am certain that there has been some mistake," she said stiffly, continuing toward the door. "My brother will be in touch with you and you may explain yourself to him."

"Ah, but he already understands me, Lady Diana. It is to you that I must explain myself."

"Doubtless this is a private joke, sir, one that is in extraordinarily poor taste. I certainly do not wish for you to explain it to me. I assure you that there is no need." She opened the door to leave the room.

"Very well, ma'am," he returned, finally rising and offering another brief, almost insolent, bow. "I shall be happy to explain matters to your aunt since your brother is not present and you do not wish to see me."

"Aunt Lavinia?" she said blankly, turning back to him. "Why would you wish to see her?"

"Why, to share my happy news with her so that she can welcome me into the family," he responded, smiling. "Someone needs to tell her what is taking place."

Diana shut the door and turned to face him. "You are no gentleman, sir! Why would you behave in such a manner? You must know that such an announcement would quite overset her."

He inclined his head. "As you so aptly remarked, I am no gentleman, and so I am not hampered by a gentleman's rules."

"If I were a man, I'd call you out!" she snapped, her color mounting.

"And if you were a man, I would be glad to accept your challenge," he returned, smiling at her intensity. This was the reaction he had half expected from her brother last night. "As it is, I shall marry you instead."

"You will do no such thing!" she announced, for the moment quite forgetting the wager.

"I am afraid that you will have to confer with your brother about that," he replied smoothly. "And I believe you will find that you have no choice but to marry me—it is a debt of honor that your brother must pay. And since he is a gentleman," and his tone became slightly drier at the word, "he by all means must do the honorable thing."

She turned toward the door again, then thought of what her poor aunt's reaction would be should she be called to the drawing room to face Melville—and of the call that Trevor was presently paying upon Appelby to secure his bride. This was no time to give way to temper. With a visible stiffening, she controlled her momentary burst of angry pride at his cavalier treatment and, to his surprise, seated herself once again and spoke to him quite calmly.

"Perhaps you should explain to me the terms of the wager, Mr. Melville." Having begun by acting as though she had no knowledge of the affair, she must continue the charade—and perhaps, she thought, she could turn it to her own advantage. She watched him carefully.

Melville, who had fully expected her to leave the room in angry tears and demand an explanation of Landford, explained the bet as baldly as possible, determined to let her see how her brother had betrayed her. His object, after all, had been to teach the young earl a salutary lesson in the ways of the world. His sister might as well be schooled in the same hard manner. She would soon see that her brother did not care for her above himself, that self-interest would always strangle love.

"Your brother wishes to marry Lady Genevieve," he began, and Diana nodded.

"Of course he does," she responded. "We are aware of that—and of the fact that he must have a hundred thousand pounds in order to do so."

A little taken aback by her knowledge and her matter-of-fact attitude, Melville continued. "Then you must know, of course, that your brother has no way to secure that money until he comes of age and that Lord Appelby plans to marry his daughter to another man who is able to supply that amount immediately."

Again Diana nodded, watching him closely. She smiled to herself, more certain now of her ground. Melville was attempting to shock her, to show her that Trevor cared only for himself. For reasons of his own, he was attempting to drive a wedge between her and her brother. She would not show by the flicker of an eyelash that he could do so.

"My brother has been distraught over that matter, of course," she replied. "That undoubtedly is what led him to gamble with you."

Melville paused. Whatever he had expected, it had not been calmness. "Perhaps you will not be surprised to learn, Lady Diana, that he lost that amount instead of winning it."

Diana turned the topaz ring on her finger, holding it up to the light for a moment as though she were completely absorbed in its tawny glow. Finally glancing up, she cast him what she hoped was a suitably careless smile.

"Not at all," she murmured, still twisting the ring. "Trevor has always considered himself a better player than he actually is. Is that when he wagered me—after you had driven him to the wall?"

"Yes. He was willing to sacrifice you in order to win Lady Genevieve," said Melville bluntly, watching her face closely.

Diana's carefully schooled countenance did not change. "Of course he was anxious both to secure Lady Genevieve and to regain the money lost to you—which I am certain you know he could not have paid. The predicament in which you placed him was a most unhappy one."

"You mistake matters, ma'am," Melville replied, his voice cold. "I did not place him in that predicament. Landford made his own choices."

Irritated by his attitude and the knowledge that she had indeed been responsible for the situation, she asked a question that had come to her suddenly. "And just how many women have you won in marriage, Mr Melville?"

Her question clearly took him off guard. "You have the honor of being the first," he responded, bowing briefly.

"A dubious honor at best," she observed, growing more cheerful when she saw she had thrown him slightly off-balance. She was never pleased to feel that she was being made the victim, and she was determined to cut the ground from beneath his feet by taking the offensive.

"Nonetheless, I suppose that I must comfort myself with that." Here she looked at him directly, her dark eyes large and challenging. "I assume that my brother *will* be able to marry Lady Genevieve?" she asked.

He nodded and pulled a folded paper from his waistcoat, which he laid before her. "I am a man of my word. Here is my cheque and a note to my banker."

Seeing that he was hoping to shock her by emphasizing the fact that she had been purchased, Diana calmly picked up the paper and held it firmly, still looking at him.

"Then I must keep my part of the bargain, must

I not, Mr. Melville? As soon as the money is in my brother's hands, we shall be married. How soon may you obtain a license? I shall of course have a few arrangements to make."

Whatever Melville had expected, it had not been this businesslike acceptance of the situation, nor this rush to consummate the bargain. Nor had he any real desire to do anything more than shock her and teach Landford a lesson—certainly he had no intention of marrying. He had expected a flood of tears and shocked recriminations; he had thought that Landford might beg him to reconsider the matter; he had imagined himself finally releasing the young woman after all concerned had seen to what depths Landford would sink to gratify himself. And, he admitted to himself, he had wished to see if he found the same appeal in the sister that he found in Landford.

"I think that we need not rush matters to that extent—" he began, but Diana, certain of her advantage now, pressed him.

"I would not have it said, sir, that my brother does not honor his debts," she said briskly. "I can be ready whenever you say the word."

"Indeed, that is not necessary, Lady Diana," he replied, beginning to be annoyed. Jack Melville was a man accustomed to controlling his situation. "I assure you—"

"Perhaps you feel that you got the bad end of the bargain," Diana cut in. She was beginning to enjoy herself. "I must admit that I was surprised by your wager. I would have thought you a more cautious man, not one who would, as my old nurse used to say, buy a pig in a poke."

Melville stared at her in consternation as she continued briskly and almost patronizingly. "I quite understand. You made the wager without having seen me, and now that you have, you wish to change your mind. It was very shortsighted of you, probably done under the influence of drink." Here she paused to eye him critically. "I would certainly think, however, that a seasoned gamester would not make such an error."

Thoroughly annoyed by her criticism and her attitude, he answered her quite sharply. "Lady Diana, my decision to delay our marriage for a few weeks has nothing to do with my—as you so delicately phrased it— with my buying 'a pig in a poke.' I have more important matters to attend to, I assure you, other than preparing for a wedding. I merely came as a courtesy to inform you of how matters stood."

Melville heard himself saying these words almost as if someone else were speaking. He had intended to do nothing more than to come here and set the cat among the pigeons by shocking Landford's sister with the truth and forcing the pair of them to look at the world as it really was. He had assumed that he would play cat-and-mouse with them for a day or two until Landford understood his point. He most certainly had no intention of marrying, and now this managing chit of a girl had placed him in the uncomfortable position of speaking of their marriage as though it might actually take place.

"Well, I must admit that I am relieved," responded Diana. "I shouldn't wish to be married to a man that was so careless in his wagers. Doubtless you were fully informed about me and my financial status before wagering, so I feel slightly better about your decision."

Glancing up sharply at the face of his fiancée, Melville caught a glimpse of what looked suspiciously like amusement. Almost, he thought, it was Landford's face. The look disappeared immediately, however, replaced by her former businesslike expression.

"I am gratified by your good opinion, ma'am," he replied, gratified by no such thing.

"Of course you will come to dinner tonight, Mr. Melville," said Diana as he rose. "Aunt Lavinia is resting now, but she will naturally be most anxious to meet you."

Melville, who could think of nothing he would less like to do than suffer through a family dinner, particularly in the present circumstances, started to shake his head, then remembered that if he came, he would have the opportunity to see Landford with his family and to observe the result of his work. And, he admitted to himself, he wished to see the boy again. It was a pity, he thought, that the sister appeared to have so little of Landford's charm. For a moment he had thought that there might be a marked resemblance that was more than physical, but her unexpected and decidedly unattractive acceptance of marriage—even in so unprepossessing a form—showed her unimaginative and quite tasteless.

"Of course," he responded, bowing. "I shall look forward to it." And he would. He was very interested to see how Landford would handle the awkwardness of this situation.

"We will look forward to seeing you at seven, then. It will be a simple family dinner, of course."

"Naturally," he responded. "Do give my regards to your brother."

"Indeed I will," she replied, her eyes bright. She had not missed his hesitation, and she was aware that such a dinner was precisely what he would normally avoid—unless he had a reason of his own for attending. She had no illusions. Jack Melville did things for his own amusement, and he expected to be amused.

As the door closed behind him, she smiled. Dinner might not go just as he expected—and he might not be the only one amused.

Nine

Dinner was all that Diana had hoped for. Trevor had arrived in the afternoon, aglow with the news that he and Jenny would be considered engaged the moment that her father had the money in his hand.

"Well, that is no sooner said than done," replied his sister crisply, drawing out the cheque and note and handing it to him. "Mr. Melville appears to be as good as his word. Here is the money."

"Melville!" exclaimed Trevor, all signs of joy immediately erased. "For a moment I had forgotten him!"

"You should not," returned Diana, seating herself casually with a book of fashion plates their aunt had been admiring. "It is because of that gentleman that you are able to marry Jenny and save her from Treffington."

"That gamester! I am astounded that you can refer to Melville as a gentleman, Di!"

"Why call him a gamester as though it is something reprehensible? Didn't we gamble ourselves in order to gain the money, Trevor? I don't think that gives us the right to judge him," she remarked quietly, looking up from her book.

He collapsed into a chair, for the moment deflated by her statement. "At least our cause was a worthy one," he muttered. "We weren't trying to do damage to someone else, as he was."

Diana did not reply, and when he finally looked up, he met her eyes a little defiantly. "Well, it's true, Di! We were trying to help Jenny—"

"And you," she interjected.

"Yes, and me," he admitted. "But what was Melville trying to do other than to hurt me by trying to make a game of you?"

"I'm not quite certain what he had on his mind," she admitted. "Perhaps you can ask him at dinner."

Trevor stared at her, thunderstruck. "Dinner! You don't mean to say that that man is coming to this house for dinner!"

"Of course he is. After all, we are—in a manner of speaking—engaged."

"You are not!" he exclaimed vehemently, jumping up to stride about the room. "You'll have nothing to do with him!"

"He has already been here and I have already spoken with him," Diana responded placidly, "and if you will calm down and listen to me, Trevor, you will see that we have him just where we want him."

Mystified by her words, he had sat down to listen. Diana related her story deftly, and she was glad to see that he was amused by her confrontation of Melville. She omitted much of that gentleman's offensive conversation, just as she had failed to tell Trevor that she had had a choice to make when she lost to Melville the night before. Some things, she decided, were simply not necessary knowledge for her brother. He was already angry enough with

Melville; if he knew the full truth, they probably would find themselves on a dueling field immediately. She had not, in fact, even told Tom the full truth about the wager.

Seeing that Trevor was now in a slightly better frame of mind at the thought of Melville being made uncomfortable, Diana ventured to add, "And so, Trev, it seems to me that we can keep the whole matter of the wager very quiet, for the man most certainly has no desire to marry. The most it will cost me is a few evenings in Mr. Melville's company. And after all, I have just arrived in London, so who is going to take note of my activities?"

"Well, that might be true," he conceded grudgingly, "but I can't bear the thought of your having to spend any time at all with such a man as that, Di."

"I assure you that I will enjoy myself," she replied, smiling to herself. "I intend to give Mr. Melville a lesson in manners. He may be accustomed to calling the tune, but he has overreached himself this time."

"So he has!" exclaimed her brother. "And if anyone can teach him that lesson, we can!"

"No, you weren't attending to me, Trev. I said that *I* will teach him the lesson. I've earned the right to do so, haven't I?" she inquired, eyeing him firmly.

He nodded, glancing down at the cheque and note in his hand. "You're right, Di. If it weren't for your getting this from Melville, I wouldn't have had a chance of marrying Jenny. I don't know how we shall ever be able to thank you."

"You would have done as much for me, Trevor," she replied, dismissing it lightly. "But tonight at din-

ner you and Tom must remember to follow my lead.
You can't take off on tangents of your own, and you
can't attack our guest. Promise me!"

He grinned at her, rumpling his hair and collaps-
ing into the nearest chair. "I promise, Di." He
looked at her for a moment, and his smile widened.
"Do you know, I almost feel sorry for Melville. He
has no idea what a mare's-nest he has stepped into."

The group that assembled for dinner was a handsome one to look at, and one would never have
guessed the wildly differing emotions behind each
polished facade. All of them were familiar with the
ways of their world and the value of self-possession,
so there was little prospect of any confrontation.
Nonetheless, trouble bubbled just below the smooth
surface of the evening.

Lady Lavinia was every inch (all sixty of them) the
lady, but she had been forced to resort secretly to
the rouge pot in order to restore the usual pink to
her plump cheeks. Although she looked immaculate, she felt that she had been plunged into an icy-
cold lake and she might never fight her way back
to the surface. How she came to be sitting down to
dinner with a man who had won her niece in a wager was quite beyond her understanding, but Diana
had told her firmly that it must be done. And how
she would ever explain to Mr. Barton the fact that
Diana had dressed up as Trevor and gone to the
man's home alone—and lost herself into the bargain—was beyond her. And then there was the matter of Trevor now being engaged to Appelby's girl

without his uncle's permission—and at the price of £100,000. There was no possible way any of it could be explained to any sensible person, and certainly not to a man like Robert Barton. Nonetheless, she thought, appearances must be preserved. No good cause would be served by flinging herself across the roast quail and asparagus upon her plate and sobbing.

Feeling that all was lost, she turned to Melville, who was seated on her right, and remarked brightly, "I understand that you served on the Continent, sir. What fascinating tales you must have to tell!"

Melville inclined his head gravely, but his eyes gleamed. He had heard enough about Lady Lavinia to know what duress she must be feeling at the moment. Indeed, she was the only one for whom he felt any real pity since she had brought none of this upon herself.

"I did indeed serve, ma'am, but I would hesitate to bore you with any of my stories. I am afraid that much of my time was spent away from actual battle."

"Plucking the local pigeons with a deck of cards," muttered Tom, who blushed furiously when he realized that everyone at the table had heard him. Throwing an apologetic glance at Diana, who had instructed him carefully about his behavior, he hurried into speech. "Doubtless some very interesting goings-on in—in—wherever you were. I've thought a bit myself about going over to France—to Paris, you know—now that Boney has been put away once and for all."

Melville shook his head. "I would not suggest that

you do so, Ralston. I doubt that you would care for it."

Tom bristled slightly at that. "And why would I not care for it, sir?" he demanded.

"Do you speak French?" inquired Melville.

"Lord, no!" exclaimed Tom, repelled by such a thought. "Why would I want to do such a thing?"

Melville smiled slightly. "It makes it easier to get along in a foreign country if you can speak the language."

"Do you mean to say that they don't speak English?" demanded his victim, shocked.

"Some of them, but they appear to think that we should know their language if we come to their country."

"And I suppose that you speak French *and* Spanish since you've spent time in both those places?" inquired Trevor as Tom retired into his wine, shaking his head over the shortcomings of the French.

Tom's eyes widened when Melville nodded briefly in answer to the question. "I learned them both when I was a boy, but it is different, of course, when you actually live in the country and speak it daily. It's best to know the ways of a country if you spend time there."

Tom and Trevor exchanged a look of disbelief at this unexpected and un-English comment. Members of the *ton* delighted in tossing about fashionable French phrases, but the majority of them expected a foreign place to adapt to them rather than the other way round, almost as if they constituted a little bit of England wherever they went.

"Daresay that's why you seem so different," observed Tom, pleased to be able to assign a cause to Melville's idiosyncrasies. "Spending all that time with all those foreigners would make its mark on a fellow."

Diana spoke before Melville could reply. "I have longed to go to Paris myself," she announced, drawing an amazed glance from her brother, who had never heard her speak of such a longing. "When do you think we shall be able to go, Mr. Melville? Perhaps I shall purchase my trousseau there."

Trevor, understanding his cue, made himself speak. "Perhaps we could make it a family party," he said with forced joviality. "Jenny and I could come—and Aunt Lavinia, of course, and Tom. We would make quite a jolly group."

Melville, who had been in the act of lifting his glass to his lips, shuddered slightly. He had a sudden mental picture of himself in Paris shepherding such a flock. There had been an influx of English sightseers after the fear of Napoleon had been laid to rest at Waterloo, and the sight of them had never failed to horrify him, for they were so obviously—and noisily—out of place in that city.

Diana's lips curved. She had seen the shudder and decided to press her advantage. "How delightful that would be!" she agreed. "Don't you think so, Tom?"

Here she turned to the hapless Tom, who had been attempting to follow the sudden turn of conversation. Since he scarcely wished to be in the same room with Melville, the thought of setting off to parts unknown with him held no appeal at all, but he understood from Diana's tone that he was expected to do his part.

"Capital!" he exclaimed, with an attempt at heartiness, seeking desperately for something he could say. He could only think of one point to contribute. "Good cooks, the Frogs. Of course," he added after a moment's earnest thought, "they slather so many dratted sauces on the food that you can't tell what's under 'em."

Being a man fond of beefsteak and rather plain fare, he warmed to his subject. "Like that cook of Rayburn's," he continued. "D' you know what he served us for dinner the other night?"

Not waiting for any of his rather startled listeners to reply, he continued with a rising sense of outrage. "I could see that it was fish, of course, but it was dressed with some gravy that made it look like it was fit for nothing but the pigs! I asked Rayburn what it was, and he started throwing French at me; but when I asked him to tell me in plain English, he said it was gravy made from the fat of a green goose!"

Here he eyed his listeners to see if they perceived the full depth of the horror of the situation. Melville's shoulders shook slightly, but no shadow of a smile showed in his response. "I can readily see, Mr. Ralston, that you would greatly enjoy a trip to Paris," he said gravely.

Tom looked at him suspiciously, but Diana spoke before he could take up his grievance again. "Naturally he would, Mr. Melville—we all would. Why, I know Aunt Lavinia has been longing to go ever since

Waterloo. She visited the Court there when she was just a girl and met the Queen."

Melville turned to Lady Lavinia with interest. "Did you indeed, ma'am?" he inquired. "I would have given much to see Paris in those days."

"It was delightful," replied that lady dreamily, forgetting for a moment that she was speaking to the author of all their troubles. "Everything looked like something from a book of my fairy tales, and Marie Antoinette was kindness itself to me."

"Was she as lovely as they say?" he asked. "I have seen portraits, of course, but I have often thought that the reports of her beauty must have been greatly exaggerated."

Lady Lavinia shook her head firmly. "No, indeed. If anything, they do not do her justice. She was beautiful, it is true—but she had a sweetness of expression that set her apart from a mere beauty." Here her eyes filled with tears. "I have often thought that if any of that heartless canaille had truly known her, they could not have treated her so cruelly."

Here she had recourse to the patch of lace that served as her handkerchief and wiped her eyes. To Diana's amazement, Melville leaned forward and took the small dimpled hand of his hostess.

"I think that if she had had you as an advocate, ma'am, she might yet survive," he said gently, no hint of mockery in his tone.

Feeling that matters were not progressing in the direction she wished—that is, in the direction of making their guest exceedingly uncomfortable—Diana decided that she needed to take charge of the conversation.

"Perhaps, Mr. Melville, you will take us to see Versailles? I should imagine that we would be able to make time for that."

To her annoyance, he ignored her and focused his attention still upon her aunt.

"Lady Lavinia," he said, his tone warm, "if you should wish to see it, I would be delighted to take you."

Lady Lavinia fluttered under such intense masculine approval, some of her natural color beginning to return. "You are very kind, sir, but I should not wish to intrude upon your time with your bride—"

She broke off as she realized what she was saying, and the appalling reality of their situation swept over her once more and she covered her lips with her free hand. Melville patted the small hand he was still holding comfortingly before withdrawing his own.

"Perhaps after that we could go on even to Switzerland and Rome, with you and Di," remarked Trevor, forcing himself to speak casually as he leaned back in his chair and surveyed his guest lazily.

"You appear to be taking your sister's marital plans very lightly, Landford," remarked Melville, studying him closely. He scarcely seemed the same young man. "I confess that you surprise me. I had expected quite another attitude."

"Indeed?" inquired Trevor, his lips thinning as he sat up a little straighter. "And just what did you expect?"

Melville shrugged. "A trace of concern, perhaps. After all, you have agreed to give me your sister in marriage, but what do you know of me aside from what little the gossips have told you?"

Lady Lavinia gasped and put her hand to her mouth once again. The day had been more than she could bear with equanimity, and she reached for her vinaigrette.

"Nothing," confessed Trevor through his teeth, wishing that he could strike the man. He maintained his unusual self-restraint only because his sister caught his eye and held it firmly.

"Just what do you feel it is necessary for him to know, Mr. Melville?" inquired Diana in an interested tone. "We are aware that you are a hardened gamester who breaks other men's fortunes without a qualm and wins your bride at cards. Now you have told us that you served in the military. What else must we know?"

There was another sharp intake of breath from Lady Lavinia as she sank back in her chair and inhaled deeply from the vinaigrette, certain that she had been plunged into a nightmare from which she would soon awaken. Tom hurried to an array of decanters on the sideboard and poured her a glass of brandy, grateful that there was no servant present at the moment to hear such outrageous conversation.

Melville regarded her quietly for a moment. "Nothing at all." He paused and his gaze turned to her brother. "If Landford is willing to relinquish you to the man you have just described, that is his affair."

Trevor half rose in his seat, but Tom, abandoning the brandy for the moment, moved quickly to his side and murmured something into his ear. The earl, still glaring at Melville, sank reluctantly back into his chair.

Melville, however, rose from his. "As you see, Lady Diana," he said dryly, "you are in admirable hands. Your safekeeping will be transferred from your brother's tender care to my own." He bowed to her, adding, "I trust you will sleep better this night for knowing it."

To Trevor, whose painful flush had faded, leaving him a deathly shade, he also bowed. "Forgive me for not remaining to join you and Lord Ralston over brandy. I am certain that your conversation will be much more enjoyable without me."

Finally he turned to Lady Lavinia, whose hand he once more took and bowed over, touching it lightly to his lips. "And I must ask your forgiveness, ma'am, for my most unforgivable behavior in your home."

At the door he paused and turned to Diana once more. "With your permission, ma'am," he announced in a voice that indicated he required no permission at all, "I shall call upon you tomorrow morning." And with a curt nod to the rest of them, he was gone.

"Well, by Jove," murmured Tom, sinking into his chair and wiping his brow with his handkerchief. "What an unbelievable fellow!"

"I should like to meet him at dawn!" said Trevor in a low voice. "What sort of brother am I that I would allow him to conduct himself in such a manner?"

"You know what is at stake," Diana reminded him crisply. "If you allow your emotions to get the best of you, Trevor, you will forfeit Jenny and ruin both of us!"

Trevor shook his head slowly. "Di, are you not listening to this man?" he asked in disbelief. "He is set to marry you. I cannot let you throw yourself away for my happiness."

"Nonsense!" she returned sharply. "He has not the slightest intention of marrying me! We talked about this before, Trev. We know that he has some sort of plan of his own—he is merely inflicting misery on both of us for his own pleasure. He would never subject himself to marrying me simply because he wants to teach you a lesson. You saw his reaction when he thought he might have to escort all of us to his precious Paris."

An audible sigh from their aunt attracted their attention, and Diana hurried to her side and embraced her. "And, my dear Aunt, however can we apologize to you for having you undergo such a dreadful evening?"

"Actually," murmured their aunt, still waving the vinaigrette feebly beneath her nose, "I think Mr. Melville is a fine figure of a man—and so sympathetic, too. Perhaps, my dears, this will all work out for the best."

Ten

Diana was not at all pleased the following morning when her first two visitors, arriving long before good taste dictated, were announced and took up residence in the drawing room, with the firm determination of remaining there for the duration of the day if necessary.

"I won't have you facing him alone," said Trevor flatly, settling himself with the attitude of one who was prepared to make whatever sacrifices necessary.

"Certainly not," agreed Tom, ensconcing himself firmly in a corner of the sofa and hoping devoutly that Melville would have found some new interest that would keep him away and allow them to return to their lives. Like Lady Lavinia, he felt that his life had become a walking nightmare from which he must soon be delivered.

"Don't be ridiculous," replied Diana impatiently—and without a trace of proper gratitude, thought Tom bitterly. "If you two are here, I won't be able to find out the things that I need to know."

They both stared at her.

"What things?" demanded her brother. "What do you think you can learn from him except your wedding date?"

Diana grinned. "Precisely which things annoy him most."

"What do you mean by that?" asked Trevor suspiciously. "Is this more of your attempt to have him cry off?"

"Naturally. By the time I have done with Mr. Melville, he will be grateful to be able to walk away from his bartered bride." She did not add that she would enjoy the whole experience. Last night as Lady Diana, she had missed the unexpected closeness she had felt to him when she was the Earl of Landford, and she meant to reestablish it. Jack Melville's appeal was growing stronger. He was a most fascinating man, and she thought with satisfaction of the coming battle with him.

Her brother was not appeased, however. "That's just fine, Di! I'm supposed to allow you to prance around London with such a fellow as that without saying a word! I think you can probably manage him very well if anyone can do so, but everyone else will think that I am beef-witted for letting my sister be in his company!"

He sat and reflected bitterly for a moment. "And Lord knows what they would say if they knew the truth!" He and Tom both shuddered, but Diana chuckled.

"You are refining upon this far too much, Trev. No one is going to know save our little circle, and when all is said and done, you will be able to marry Jenny and no one will have come to harm over it—except perhaps Mr. Melville."

"And so he should!" exclaimed the earl. "He deserves whatever misery you can deal him, Di!"

Tom was a little more hesitant about this. Having himself been subjected to Diana's whims, he felt that perhaps his friend was being a trifle harsh with Melville. However, after a moment of consideration, he decided that Melville would have to take his chances.

"Hear, hear!" he exclaimed, raising his empty hand in a mock toast. "To the downfall of the enemy!"

"I do hope that you are not referring to me." Melville stood in the doorway, stripping off his gloves, while the butler, his expression desperate, edged by him.

"Mr. Melville," Tibbett announced briefly and fled.

"A fine sort of butler," muttered Trevor. "Doubtless he'd let in all the scaff and raff of the street if we would allow it."

Melville regarded him with some amusement. "I do hope that you're not referring to me, too, Landford. My behavior may not be precisely *de rigueur,* but I have never considered myself the 'scaff and raff of the street.' "

"I daresay not," agreed Tom, nodding knowledgeably before Trevor could speak, "but then the scaff and raff probably don't think of themselves in those terms either."

Melville paused and stared at Tom a moment before giving a shout of laughter, a response that left Tom totally bewildered. "I must congratulate you, Landford," he said. "You must choose your friends for their candor and their ability to amuse."

Tom looked slightly offended. "I had no intention of amusing," he replied stiffly.

"Well, of course you didn't, Tom," agreed Trevor patiently. "That's what he means, you see."

Tom, who did not see, looked bewildered and still somewhat annoyed.

Here Melville turned to Diana, who had been wondering whether or not he had heard Trevor's remark about dealing him as much misery as possible. His expression as he met her eyes after bending low over her hand did not reveal his thoughts. He still looked amused, she thought, half-amused herself but annoyed by his ease in what she had hoped to make an awkward situation.

"I am delighted to see you looking so well, ma'am," he drawled, his green eyes fixed upon her.

"You speak as though you expected to find me looking otherwise, sir," she replied, trying unsuccessfully to withdraw her hand from his.

"You must admit that many young ladies of a more delicate constitution than your own would find your situation very distressing," he said. "Some, indeed, would take to their beds over far less than this."

"As you see, sir, I am made of sterner stuff than those young ladies you mention," returned Diana dryly. "I see that you admire milk-and-water misses— I fear that is not what you will be getting in me."

"I should say not!" exclaimed Tom fervently. "Milk and water!" He had begun a most ungentlemanly chortle when he was suddenly aware that the other three were looking at him in some astonishment. Blushing, he added hurriedly to

Melville, "Lady Diana is not just in the common style, you see."

Melville's lips curved into a semblance of a smile. "I had begun to guess as much, Mr. Ralston. I am grateful to have you confirm my opinion."

Tom nodded seriously, careful not to meet the eyes of Diana or his friend. "You will find her exceptional and—" He paused, searching for an appropriate word. "And unexpected," he concluded with satisfaction.

"Well, ma'am," murmured Melville, turning once again to Diana, "this is high praise indeed. I do so dislike being bored. Lord Ralston's reassurance on that point is gratefully received."

Her eyes glittered dangerously. "I am, of course, most eager for your good opinion, sir," she said, her tone belying her words.

Melville looked at her quizzically. "An interesting comment, my lady," he murmured, "and I am overwhelmed by the sincerity of your tone. I would not have expected that reaction of you, so Mr. Ralston's observation must be correct."

"I do not see how you know me well enough to know what to expect of me," she returned stiffly.

"Ah, but I have the advantage of you there, you see, for I asked your brother a good many questions about you during our evenings together."

Diana's eyes flew to those of her brother, whose expression had darkened ominously. Before he could say anything, she spoke quickly. "Yes, I had quite forgotten that Trevor told me about your inquiries."

"Did he indeed?" inquired Melville curiously,

glancing at Trevor. "I knew that twins are reputed to have an unusual bond, but I see that the two of you are even closer than I had thought."

Here Tom, thinking of Diana's masquerade, choked perceptibly on his coffee, his eyes watering and his face turning scarlet.

"You had best get him something to drink and walk him about outside, Trevor," Diana commanded briskly. "He appears to be falling into one of his spells."

Trevor, although unwilling either to be commanded or to leave her alone with Melville, recognized the imminent danger of Tom giving everything away. Once he was overset, as he clearly was now, he was capable of any indiscretion. Thinking of Jenny, Trevor reluctantly escorted the maligned Tom from the room, throwing a cautionary glance at his sister before closing the door behind them.

"Now that we are private, sir," Diana said crisply, "we may get down to the business at hand. May I ask if you have sent the announcement of our engagement to the paper yet?"

"Doing so seemed a trifle premature," he responded, his tone distant. Obviously he had no wish to discuss a matter that would publicly commit him to marriage.

Pleased to see that she had managed to elicit an uncomfortable response, she pressed her advantage. Tormenting Mr. Melville promised to be most enjoyable.

"I fear that you will think me presumptuous then," she murmured, glancing down at her skirt and smoothing a wrinkle demurely, happy to avoid his eyes for a moment.

"And why should I think that?" he asked sharply.

"Why, I wrote an announcement yesterday," she replied, "for I have always found that unpleasant duties should be faced at once."

"And did you send it?" he demanded, moving closer and attempting to look her in the eye.

Diana continued to smooth the wrinkle studiously until he cupped his hand under her chin and forced her to look up at him. "Would that be so very terrible, Mr. Melville?" she inquired gently, forcing herself not to react to his unexpected movement. "After all, we are engaged, are we not?"

He ignored her second question, for a sudden idea had surfaced conveniently—one that would spare him further conversations on this subject with her.

"You forget, ma'am, that I must ask your uncle's permission before taking such a public step," he replied smoothly.

Her first reaction to his hand under her chin had been to strike it away, but two things stopped her: the memory of what she was trying to accomplish, and the arresting depth of his green eyes.

"And you forget yourself, sir, to make so free with me," Diana responded automatically, still looking into his eyes. "Perhaps you mistake me for one of your flirts."

"Not at all," said Melville, putting his free arm around her waist and pulling her from her chair. "Those ladies do not make the mistake of attempting to rule me. And there is another difference."

"What may that be?" she asked, holding his gaze and attempting to remain nonchalant even though she was now firmly pressed against him and only a feather's depth remained between their lips.

"They are less costly," he murmured, kissing her soundly and holding her tightly as she struggled in his arms.

When she managed to free herself, Diana slapped him resoundingly. "You are not talking to some bit of muslin, sir!" she fumed.

"Precisely my point, ma'am," he replied in amusement, "although I confess I am shocked at your use of such a term. You have been in your brother's company too much. That is something that I will see to once we are married."

He saw with satisfaction that fury at his remark had left her virtually speechless as she turned toward the window. Two could play at this game, he thought, amused by her attempts to bait him.

Diana struggled with herself as she clutched the drape and stared out the window at the passing carriages. Having taken the liberty of kissing her in such a manner was bad enough, but to have him intimate that, were they to marry, he would control her actions to the point that he would keep her from seeing Trevor was too much to bear.

Seeing her brother pacing back and forth with Tom on the pavement below recalled her to a sense of her duty in this matter. She could not give way to temper. She must remember Trevor's marriage to his Jenny.

As she drew a deep breath and grew calmer, she realized suddenly that his remark about Trevor had also indicated that he would marry her—doubtless that had escaped his attention in his eagerness to aggravate her. And, she thought with a quick rush of pleasure, that was precisely what he had wished to do—aggravate her. He was trying to do the same thing that she was.

Turning from the window, she determined to carry the war into the enemy's territory. "You are quite right, of course, Mr. Melville," she said with deceptive gentleness. "We must ask Uncle Robert's permission. I shall write to him immediately."

There was a brief but perceptible pause. When she glanced up, his eyes were glinting brightly—rather like those of a cat about to pounce, she thought.

"Do not trouble yourself, Lady Diana. I shall take care of my own affairs." He bowed briefly, then turned toward the door. "And I shall call for you at eight tonight," he announced. "I believe that it is time that we spent an evening together without the company of your family."

Imagining suddenly that he might take her to some such place as Le Chateau Royale, thinking to make her feel like one of the high-fliers she had seen there, set her instantly on her guard.

"I trust, sir, that we will not go to a public place such as the theatre, or—" Here she feigned distress, forcing her eyes to fill with fear.

"Or?" he inquired briskly.

"Certainly not to a private party where we would encounter any ladies that might later recognize me," she faltered. "After all, what might they think of my poor brother for letting me go out with you unescorted?"

She saw with satisfaction that her point had been made. "I think, Lady Diana, that you should become accustomed to such difficulties—and certainly your brother must. We shall attend Lady Sotheby's rout this evening."

Before she could respond, he had gone. Thoughtfully she watched as he descended the front steps and stopped to speak to Trevor and Tom. The interchange was brief, and Melville went striding down the street, leaving the other two looking after him.

An evening alone with Jack Melville! He had no way of knowing, of course, that they had spent the evening together before. Diana smiled to herself with satisfaction. It would be an enjoyable time—she would see to that. He was doubtless annoyed with himself for saying that he would write to Uncle Robert, and she intended to make the most of that sore point.

She touched her lips lightly, thinking of his kiss. A strange thing, she thought, that he had shown a marked fondness for Landford, but seemed to feel so little for her as the victim. He had kissed her not for the pleasure of doing so, but for the power it gave him over her. It had been to put her in her place.

She smiled. Tom would have felt distinctly unwell had he been there, for he would have recognized its ominous quality. It was, she thought, high time that someone put Mr. Melville firmly into his own place.

Eleven

Trevor was naturally beside himself when he learned that Melville had announced that he would be escorting her to an evening party.

"The confounded fellow said as coolly as you please that the two of you would be attending Lady Sotheby's rout tonight! How could you let him do such a thing, Di?" he demanded.

She shook her head. "Mr. Melville was quite firm," she remarked. "I believe that this is to be a warning to us."

Whatever his plans, Melville undoubtedly meant for her to be made uncomfortable. And poor Trevor, of course, was already distraught. Melville was doing his work all too well.

A few minutes of conversation, however, helped Trevor come to grips with the problem. After all, she pointed out calmly, he and Jenny and Tom would also be present at that evening party. This observation had the happy effect of diverting his attention to his fiancée.

"You will be able to meet her tonight, Di!" he exclaimed. "And her father has promised that I may bring her here to meet Aunt Lavinia as soon as possible. You will love her, I know—she is an angel!"

"I am certain that I shall love her immediately," she assured her brother, grateful that his thoughts had taken this cheerful turn. And, considering for a moment his remark about their aunt, she too brightened. "And I think it only right that Aunt Lavinia meet her at the same time," she added. "I shall send a note round to Mr. Melville at once, telling him that Lady Lavinia will be accompanying us this evening. You saw how he behaved with her last night. If she is dressed and waiting with me this evening, he will not forbid her to come with us."

Trevor grinned. "I'd give a monkey to see his face when he reads that note. He certainly got more than he bargained for when he won you, Di!"

His smile faded at his own words. "Just listen to what I said," he sighed. "I'm speaking of this wager as though it were the most natural thing in the world instead of the disgrace that it is."

"Don't fall into the mopes, Trevor," replied his sister bracingly. "First of all, you aren't responsible for the bet—and aren't we doing very well with this so far? You have Jenny and we know that poor Melville has no real desire to marry anyone, least of all me. And tonight I shall be well chaperoned by our aunt."

"And I will be there, too," announced Tom stoutly. "You have only to give me a sign and I shall be at your side, Di."

To his dismay, Diana kissed him on the cheek. "Thank you for being such a good friend, Tom. I assure you that you may both enjoy your evening. I shall be perfectly fine with Aunt."

She certainly had not the least intention of telling

either of them about Melville's presumptuous kiss.
She hugged the memory of it to her. He would not
attempt any such liberty with Aunt Lavinia present
that evening, and she realized that she felt almost
regretful at the thought. This will never do, she
thought, shaking her shoulders firmly. She must remember that she was engaged in the business of
frightening him away, not anchoring him in place.

Lady Lavinia was all aflutter when it was time for
Melville to arrive. She had adjusted her gown carefully and made countless journeys to the glass to pat
the filmy bit of lace on her head.

"You look very fetching, Aunt," Diana reassured
her after one such journey. "And you have already
made a conquest of him—that was clear enough last
night."

"What nonsense you talk, child!" she replied,
flushing. "It's no such thing and you know it!"

"Indeed I don't know it," responded her niece,
smiling. "His liking for you almost makes me reconsider my opinion of Mr. Melville. After all, anyone
with a fondness for you must have some redeeming
characteristics."

"You are foolish beyond permission," said Lavinia, frowning. "Although I must confess that he
seems very much the gentleman. I find it difficult
to credit that he did such a reprehensible thing as
to win you in a card game. Are you quite sure that
is the way it went, my dear?"

Then, looking at her niece's expression, she nodded. "Forgive me, Diana. I keep forgetting that you

were there instead of Trevor." Here her lower lip quivered. "If your uncle ever hears of this matter, I shall nevermore be allowed to live with you."

Diana enfolded her in her arms. "Don't think of such a thing, Aunt. No one will be permitted to take you away from us."

Melville, who had once again evaded the butler, stood in the doorway as she said this. Without being seen, he retreated once more into the passageway and thrust the butler ahead of him.

"Mr. Melville!" bleated Tibbett, then backed hurriedly from the room.

"Ladies," he murmured, bowing low. "You are a vision of loveliness. I am a most fortunate man to escort two such beauties."

Lady Lavinia blushed as he leaned over her hand and kissed it. "It was very kind of you to include me in your invitation, Mr. Melville."

His glance slid to Diana, who smiled at him pleasantly as he murmured, "I assure you that it was my pleasure, ma'am."

His gentlemanly demeanor continued for all the first portion of the evening as he settled the ladies in comfortable chairs and retrieved refreshments for them. Then Lady Lavinia was delighted to see two of her old friends, and she promptly disappeared with them into the card room.

Melville, taking immediate advantage of the moment, steered Diana down a passageway and out onto a dark terrace.

"Why are we—" she began, but found herself unable to continue her question, for he had enfolded her in his arms and pressed his lips to her own. For a moment there was nothing else but the two of them, molded so closely to one another that each could feel the breathing of the other. Diana had the sudden, extraordinary sensation that she was melting, that her body had become like the melting wax of a flaming candle.

Whatever she had been expecting, it had not been this. Without the company of her aunt she would have prepared herself for such an eventuality, but having Lady Lavinia had given her what was clearly a false sense of security. Diana did not think such thoughts until later, however.

She emerged from his embrace considerably shaken, precisely as Melville had planned that she should. What he had not taken into account, however, was that he might be deeply shaken himself.

Determined that she would not give him the satisfaction of seeing his effect upon her, Diana took herself firmly in hand before speaking.

"Checking upon the value of your wager, Mr. Melville?" she inquired in a voice carefully empty of emotion. "I do hope you find me satisfactory."

Melville was still standing far too close, she thought a little nervously.

"I am not entirely certain that I did," he murmured, pulling her to him again. And once again everything seemed to stop and melt together. For the moment she would not have cared if the entire household had emptied into the garden to be their audience. Nothing could have stopped them.

A few minutes later some clarity of thought returned to her and she pulled away, chilled by the cool spring night once they had separated. "We should go in, Mr. Melville. I am cold," she said briefly, turning toward the door.

"I agree that we should go in, ma'am, but I am very far from agreeing that you are cold," he returned, following her.

Once inside, Melville escorted her to a more private corner of the room they had occupied before, chatting idly as though nothing had occurred. Indeed, in a few minutes he once more became himself entirely and moved briskly to business.

"Tell me, ma'am, about this uncle of yours," he said, moving his chair closer to hers.

"Uncle Robert?" she returned, startled.

"He is the one to whom I must write, is he not?" inquired Melville blandly, pleased that he had once again taken her unawares.

"Well, yes, of course he is. However, I thought that—" She broke off here in confusion because what she was thinking of saying was that she did not believe that Melville had any intention of asking her uncle for her hand in marriage. However, she could not say as much to him without giving herself away. Recognizing her predicament and enjoying it fully, he sat back and left her to flounder.

"I thought that you had his direction," she managed finally, refusing to meet his eyes.

"No, I'm afraid that I haven't had the pleasure of meeting that gentleman, or even of knowing his name beyond 'Uncle Robert'; and I daresay—quite aside from the fact that a letter with such a brief direction would not arrive at the proper destination—that he would prefer that I not address him so informally before I am made a member of the family."

Diana had a brief mental image of her uncle's reaction should Melville take such a liberty, and she laughed reluctantly. "No," she agreed, "that would be most unwise. Uncle Robert—Mr. Robert Barton—is quite a formal gentleman."

"Even with you and your brother?" he asked curiously.

"Especially with us," she replied dryly. "And with Aunt Lavinia. He thinks that all of us are too light-minded. I am certain that if you ask to pay your addresses to me, he will forewarn you of my many weaknesses and assure you that you would be better off to marry someone of sturdier character."

"You make him sound most unappealing," Melville observed. "Perhaps it would be better if I saw him in person rather than writing to him."

Diana stared at him. He was behaving for all the world as though he had every intention of actually speaking with Uncle Robert and asking to marry her. She was displeased to note that her heart was beating faster at that thought, and it was not because she found the prospect completely distasteful.

"Oh, I think Uncle Robert is fully capable of refusing just as promptly in person as he is in a letter," she said casually. "In fact, I am quite certain that if he should receive a letter, he would feel it his obligation to come immediately to London to do just that, so you would see him in any case."

She shuddered as she thought of his coming. He would doubtless descend upon them like a cold north wind, finding ways to make their lives miserable and to keep Trevor from marrying Jenny. Just the thought of it made her grit her teeth in anger.

"I see that he is quite a favorite," remarked Melville, who had been watching her with interest. Teaching young Landford a lesson was proving to be more complicated than he had at first anticipated. The sister obviously had an agenda of her own and was attempting to unsettle him by pressing the matter of marriage. It was a game, he reflected grimly, at which two could play, although he had to admit to himself that their encounter in the garden had left him most unsettled—a reaction that he had not counted upon. And Lady Lavinia was proving to be an unanticipated problem. He had no wish to victimize her, and the bit of conversation he had overheard that morning indicated that he would be.

Before she could answer, Trevor swept down upon them. "Di, this is Lady Genevieve—Jenny!" If he had just announced the Queen, he could not have looked more proud.

Diana rose laughing and took the hand of the fragile-looking girl he bore upon his arm. "I am so very glad to meet you, my dear," she said warmly. "Trevor has been singing your praises ever since we arrived in London."

Lady Genevieve colored deeply, the flush in sharp contrast to her ivory skin and pale, fair curls. "And he has told me all about you, Lady Diana," she said, her voice very soft and low.

"Well, you must not believe him," returned Diana. "I am not nearly as shocking as he paints me."

Lady Genevieve looked distressed and colored

more deeply still. "Oh, but I didn't mean—" she began, but Trevor interrupted, laughing.

"Don't mind her, Jenny. She is funning, you see."

Lady Genevieve looked relieved but also puzzled. Melville, watching the scene closely, was surprised to see that Landford's choice was quite so literal-minded. He would have expected the boy to select someone a little quicker, but then she was undeniably lovely—and that was undoubtedly all that the boy saw.

Diana, suddenly remembering her companion, said quickly, "And I should like for you to meet Mr. Melville, Lady Genevieve."

Melville bowed to her. "Your servant, ma'am," he said quietly. Then, catching Landford's eye, he looked at the boy quizzically.

Trevor immediately looked restive. "Where is Aunt Lavinia, Di? I thought that she would be here with you."

"She is—or at least she is presently in the card room. Mr. and Mrs. Samson are here, you see."

"We'll just go along and find them then," he announced, anxious to remove Jenny from Melville's vicinity. "Forgive us for leaving you, Di," he murmured, throwing a dark glance at her companion. "We'll be back shortly."

She watched them thread their way through the crowd, a smile lingering on her lips.

"Does it not trouble you?" asked Melville abruptly.

"Doesn't what trouble me?" she asked. "That my brother is happy?"

"That he is happy at your expense," he replied

impatiently. "Just look at him—leading away the young woman that he will marry, having sold you and your own prospects for happiness in order to do so."

Diana turned away from him. "You don't know my brother," she said stiffly. "You misjudge him."

Melville caught her elbow and forced her to face him. "You're wrong," he replied quietly. "I do know him. You forget **that I was there w**hen he talked of you and when **he so easily let you be the subject** of our wager—all for t**he sake of his own happiness.**"

"As I said, Mr. Melville, you do not know my brother. I must ask you not to speak of him in such a manner." She glanced down at his hand, which still held her elbow firmly. "And I would appreciate it, sir, if you would release me. I am not yet your property."

As soon as he removed his hand, she slipped into the crush of people surrounding them. Cursing, he attempted to follow her, but she was making her way too quickly for him to catch her before she reached the ballroom.

Pleased to have put a little distance between them, Diana paused for a moment to watch the couples waltzing to a lilting melody. She had learned the steps to the new and daring dance craze, but she had yet to try them with anyone aside from Trevor and Tom.

"May I have this dance, madam?" inquired a cool voice at her shoulder.

A tall, thin man in old-fashioned evening dress and powdered hair bowed and extended his hand, on one finger of which was a heavy gold ring fashioned like a coiled serpent with a ruby eye.

Glancing over her shoulder, Diana saw Melville bearing down upon them. Smiling warmly into the face of her rescuer, she took his hand and stepped onto the dance floor.

"I don't believe that we have met, sir," she said as he swept her gracefully into the dance. "I am—"

"You are Lady Diana Ballinger," he replied, finishing her sentence smoothly. "I have had the pleasure of meeting your brother."

"Indeed?" she remarked, smiling. "And you are—"

"Lord Treffington," he answered promptly, smiling a little grimly as her eyebrows flew up. "Indeed, ma'am, I am that very man that would have married Lady Genevieve were it not for Lord Landford's interference." The dark eyes, too closely set together in his narrow face, made him look for all the world like a bird of prey.

"You forget, sir, that you are speaking of my brother," she said stiffly, wondering if she should leave him standing on the dance floor. A glance at the crowd, however, revealed Melville, who was scowling darkly at them. She smiled to herself. If he did not wish her to dance with Treffington, she would of course do so, and leaving her unpleasant partner standing on the dance floor was no longer an option.

"Is it so very terrible that you will not marry Lady Genevieve?" she inquired soulfully, changing her tone so abruptly that he stared at her. "After all, she is not the only young woman in the *ton*."

To her dismay, Treffington tightened his grip on her waist and pulled her slightly toward him. "Quite right, Lady Diana," he murmured, gazing so intently into her eyes that she looked away. "And not all the young ladies must be paid for. Some even bring a handsome dowry to the wedding."

The old goat! she thought indignantly. Buying himself a young and beautiful bride was doubtless the only way he would acquire one. She did not allow herself to say as much, however, for she saw Melville threading his way toward them across the dance floor.

"Surely, sir, you must know what it is to win hearts," she heard herself saying. And surely he must, she thought, if only by virtue of watching other men do it.

"It is possible I have left a trail of broken hearts," he began, ready to indulge himself with a story or two. His moment did not come, however.

"I am certain that you have done precisely that, Treffington," said Melville dryly, placing his hand on Diana's arm with a proprietary air that was not lost upon her partner. "You have caused pain for many a feminine heart—but because you ruined a father or a brother or a sweetheart, not because they were yearning for you."

"Melville!" he exclaimed, his voice shaking with anger. "What are you doing here—and how dare you interfere with our dance? Who has given you authority over Lady Diana?"

A very good question, thought Diana indignantly, pleased though she was to be delivered from

Treffington. And if he did not answer carefully, all would be over for all of them.

"I am certain that I speak for Landford when I say that he would prefer that his sister have no dealings with you, Treffington," replied Melville matter-of-factly, quite as though he were telling the man that they would meet for dinner at eight.

Treffington managed to control the shaking in his voice, but it was an effort. "You are offensive, Melville!" he said sharply. "There is nothing of the gentleman in your manner!"

"And very little of it in yours," returned Melville cheerfully. "Would you like to call me out, Treffington? Pistols at dawn?"

Treffington blanched. "You know that such behavior is not allowed by the law any longer."

"Well, there is no need for the law to know, is there? We can make our own arrangements. Others have, you know."

One glance at Treffington's expression told Diana that he did indeed know but that he had no desire to do so. Bowing stiffly, he said, "Forgive me, Lady Diana. We must finish our dance another time—when we will not be so rudely disturbed." And turning abruptly, he left.

"Have you no sense of propriety?" Melville demanded in a low voice as he guided her back toward the room where they had had refreshments. "Why were you dancing—and dancing a waltz, of all things—with that man?"

Diana, who had been repelled by Treffington and grateful to be rescued, answered frostily, "I cannot see what that has to do with you, Mr. Melville."

"You are forgetting, madam, that I am soon to be your husband," he responded sharply, his voice still low.

Diana, who had for the moment forgotten that, glanced up at him quickly and then down again. He was undeniably angry—the tone of his voice and the look in his eye both told the same tale. He had fallen squarely into the trap. She smiled to herself. Doubtless his strong sense of ownership had spurred him into action against Treffington.

Using the ploy she had used effectively upon every male she had ever dealt with, she caused the tears to begin to trickle down her cheeks. "You must forgive me, Mr. Melville," she said in a brokenhearted voice. "You are quite correct, of course. I am afraid that for the moment I forgot myself."

At the sight of her tears, Melville hurried her behind a potted palm and handed her a handkerchief. "Remember where you are, ma'am," he said icily. "A rout is scarcely the place to become a watering-pot."

"Oh, and you are so absolutely correct again, Mr. Melville," she murmured into his handkerchief, taking some pleasure in blowing her nose into it. "I can't think what came over me."

Placing her hand upon his sleeve, she looked up into his eyes. "I know, sir, that I can rely upon you to show me how to be a good wife. Dare I hope that we will set the date soon?"

"There's no need for that," he replied in irritation, trying to decide what to do with the damp piece of linen she had handed back to him and recognizing the total lack of sincerity in her tone. "I still must write to your uncle before we take any definite action."

Diana reflected with satisfaction that, if his voice and expression were any indication, he would doubtless take his time about contacting her uncle. And she had discovered his intense dislike of Treffington. All in all, it had been a most useful—and eventful—evening.

"I noticed something that surprised me when you addressed Lord Treffington, Mr. Melville," she murmured, her hand still upon his arm. "I must confess it took me unawares."

"And what was that, ma'am?" inquired Melville, clearly not interested.

"Why, you accused him of breaking hearts among the ladies by ruining the men that they loved, did you not?"

"You know that I did," he returned briefly, suddenly certain of her next comment.

"And is that not precisely what you do, Mr. Melville?" she inquired sweetly, removing her hand from his sleeve. "And, if so, just how are you any different from Lord Treffington?"

"I am certain, Lady Diana," he said sharply, taking her hand before she could turn away, "that you imagine you have just delivered the *coup de grâce*. Would it not distress you," he inquired, pulling her closer to him, "to know that I agree with you?"

"And why should I be distressed because you acknowledge the truth, sir?" she asked, trying unobtrusively to slip from his grasp, which tightened as she did so.

"I thought you quicker than that, ma'am," he observed, his lips so close to her ear that his warm breath stirred her dark ringlets. "Your brother rescued his lady from Treffington, but he is perfectly willing to sacrifice you to my tender mercies. Do you not find that striking?"

He traced the line of her cheek with a caressing finger before she could pull herself away. Angry though she was, she realized that she had cornered herself. She could not defend Trevor, who was innocent of such a charge, without giving herself away. She had no choice but to continue the cat-and-mouse game with Melville until her brother was safely married.

Smiling gently at him, she replied, "Perhaps that is why I find Treffington such an attractive man, Mr. Melville—because he reminds me so much of you. I do so look forward to our wedding."

His expression was reward enough. This was, she thought, proving to be a little more wearing than she had at first anticipated. Jack Melville was in every way a worthy adversary.

Twelve

The following day did not begin auspiciously for Diana, for she received a large bouquet of blood red hothouse roses from Treffington. The card noted his hope of seeing her again in more favorable—and private—circumstances. Since the thought of seeing him again curdled her blood, Diana was at first inclined to have the roses thrown onto the rubbish heap. Upon reflection, however, she decided that she would leave them out along with the card, which bore the distinctive Treffington seal. After all, Melville would undoubtedly call, and she looked forward to seeing his expression when he realized the source of the flowers, placed judiciously next to his bouquet of daisies and yellow roses.

Melville's day began equally inauspiciously. He had returned from an early morning ride in the park—the nearest thing he could manage to a dawn ride in the country—to clear his head, only to find Burbage awaiting him with a solemn expression.

"Out with it, man!" he exclaimed, tossing down his gloves and beginning to peel his jacket off.

"Carefully, sir, carefully!" replied the valet, distressed by such cavalier treatment of a jacket tailored by Weston, which had been carefully molded to

Melville's frame. He hurried over to rescue the jacket and spent the next few moments examining it carefully for damage. "You really must be more careful, sir," he said reproachfully.

"What do you have to tell me, Burbage?" he demanded. "I saw your long face as I came through the door, and that was before I did violence to your precious jacket."

"You have a letter, sir," Burbage replied solemnly, pointing to a chest in the corner where a letter lay on a silver tray.

Melville stared at the creamy square of paper for a moment, his face tight. "From my mother, is it?" he asked.

Burbage nodded. "I'm sorry, sir," he said gently. "May I bring you something?"

"It's no matter, Burbage—nothing to be sorry about, at any rate. I'm certain that she is merely lacking in funds once again." Since the death of his father, he had heard quite regularly from his mother, who was now living an elegant life in Italy. And it was always when she was in need of money. Bitter though he was over her abandonment of him as a child, he had never been able to refuse her requests.

He slit the letter open with a silver knife and skimmed it quickly, then tossed it back onto the tray while his valet watched him anxiously.

"Money, of course," he said briefly. "And she did ask, as an afterthought, whether I was well. At least she has never asked if she is named in my will."

He turned and smiled at his valet. "You needn't

look so bleak, Burbage. No one has died, and Lord knows I am able to send her the money."

Burbage nodded, but his eyes were sad. He had served his master since Melville was a boy, and loved him despite his abrupt manners. He had been the soul of kindness to Burbage, helping him even when the valet's sister had fallen ill and had needed medical care she was unable to afford.

"Of course, sir," he said gently. "Shall I take care of it for you?"

Melville nodded. "Just send a message to Miles Stanley. He will see to it."

How simple it was for his mother, he thought. She had always enjoyed every moment of life, and she clearly had felt not the slightest trace of guilt for anything she had or had not done for her son. And since he had come into his fortune, she had felt not the slightest qualm in calling upon him for anything she needed—and she needed a good many things. Her invitation to visit her in Rome was always open to him, but he had never seen her, not since she left him as a child.

"Do you know, Burbage," he mused, regarding the toe of one highly polished riding boot thoughtfully, "I think perhaps it is easier for women to divest themselves of all conscience than it is for men."

Burbage, who knew better than to contradict his master when he was merely thinking aloud in such a bleak mood, merely made comforting noises, trying not to think of what his own sister would have to say to such a remark.

"I suppose we have brought that upon ourselves, however," he continued. "Since they have few powers of their own, undoubtedly they feel they must take advantage of us in every way possible. It is like a war."

Here he thought of Diana, and he smiled. "Of course, at times it can be a very pleasant war, Burbage."

Relieved by his master's smile, the valet smiled, too. All too often a letter from his mother requesting funds could plunge the household into a dark mood for days.

"What did you think of young Landford, Burbage?" he demanded suddenly.

Thrown slightly off-balance by the sudden change of topic, his valet paused a moment, thinking. "He seemed a very pleasant young man, sir," he offered diffidently.

"Well, yes, of course he was pleasant," replied Melville crossly. "But even a murderer may be pleasant. Did you not notice anything more particular than that?"

Burbage gave the matter a little more thought. He had traveled through the war years with his master, and often enough Melville had asked him his opinion of the men that he served during an evening. "You have a good eye for humankind, Burbage," he had said upon more than one occasion, and the valet had treasured the confidence in his judgment that his master had shown. Accordingly, he thought about young Landford more carefully. The entire household had been struck by the privacy of their master's meetings with him, and Burbage had been subjected to a barrage of questions from the other servants that he, quite naturally, had ignored.

"From what I heard while I was waiting upon you, he seems quite devoted to his family," he ventured finally, reluctant to mention the subject of family.

"Exactly!" exclaimed Melville. "And if one is devoted to his family, he does not gamble away a member of the family, does he?"

Burbage stared at him for a moment, not certain that he had understood. "The young man gambled away a member of his family, sir?" he inquired tentatively.

Melville nodded. "Landford staked his sister—or her hand in marriage, to be exact—on a game of cards with me."

Burbage felt a sudden need to sit down. His master, he knew, had ruined a number of men, had won the very roofs from over their heads, but he had never heard of his doing such a thing as winning another human being.

"I see that I have shocked you, Burbage," said Melville grimly, reaching for the brandy decanter and pouring his valet a drink. "Take this and sit down, man. I have no one else save you in whom I would confide this."

Clutching the glass of brandy like a lifeline, Burbage sat.

"A young man who loves his sister and his aunt and has no other family—except some uncle that he doesn't care for—willingly gambled away that sister in order to win the money to purchase a bride for himself!"

"To purchase a bride for himself?" inquired Burbage weakly, struggling to keep up with the tale. He had found the men his master met during wartime easier to assess as he tried to determine whether they could or could not be trusted.

"What of it, Burbage?" he asked. "Think of Portugal, think of France. If you had met young Landford there, would you have said that I could trust him?"

The valet nodded weakly. "I would have most certainly done so, sir. He seemed unaffectedly open. I must be losing my touch."

"And I must also be losing my ability to assess others," said Melville grimly. "For I would have said that he would never have done such a thing—sacrificing someone he loves for his own gratification."

"And what about the sister, sir?" inquired Burbage. "Is she distraught by the situation?"

"The sister is a managing minx—although an unusually attractive one," replied Melville grimly. "I would have said that the brother is worth a dozen of her. The chit appears to think that she can force me into marriage."

Burbage's head was whirling by this point, both with brandy and with news. "But did you not say, sir, that you won her hand in marriage?"

"I did," said his master, "but I certainly did not say that I was obliged to marry her."

Burbage stared at him. "Then what did you mean, sir?" he asked blankly.

Melville met his gaze. "I own her, Burbage," he said briefly. "It is as simple as that. I will determine whether I marry her or whether I give her in marriage to someone else."

He rose and turned his back on his valet, who was still staring at him. "I believe that I will pay a call upon the young lady, Burbage, if you will be so good as to prepare me to do so."

Burbage attempted to sort through his thoughts as he assisted his master in dressing for the morning call. All of Melville's wagers had been for horses, for land, for money—never had he made such a bet as this.

Squaring his shoulders, the valet decided that he would brave his master's displeasure and venture a question that was troubling him. "And the young lady, sir," he said as he carefully arranged the immaculate cravat, "is she angry with her brother over the wager?"

Melville snorted. "Not she! The Lady Diana professes to believe that her brother had no choice but to accept the wager. But was she overset by it? Not a bit!"

"Perhaps she is devoted to her brother, then?" suggested Burbage tentatively, straightening a last linen fold.

"They are close," he admitted, "but she seems bolder than her brother, more aggressive. And undoubtedly she would like to marry my money."

"The young lady has none of her own then?" inquired Burbage diffidently, still appearing absorbed in studying the cravat but watching his master's face carefully.

Melville blinked. "She will, I believe, have money enough when she comes of age—or when she marries." He thought for a moment. "That might explain her desire to press me into marriage," he said slowly, "except that naturally, once she marries, her money becomes her husband's—mine, to be exact."

"It could be the young lady wishes more freedom than she has," observed Burbage. He had quite liked young Landford, and he was shocked that his master had made such a tasteless wager with him.

"Possibly," agreed Melville. "Both of them appear to dislike their uncle, who manages the purse strings."

"And the lady is underage, is she not, sir? So that the uncle must approve the marriage?"

Melville nodded. "And I am quite certain that he would refuse his permission," he said. "Except that he might be grateful to have such a headache no longer his responsibility."

"And what of Lord Landford, sir?" asked Burbage, stooping to buff a rough place on the polished gloss of Melville's boots. "Does he appear distressed by the thought that his sister must marry because of the wager?"

"That's just it, Burbage," said Melville grimly, sinking back into his chair. "He is behaving precisely as I expected he would. He is completely absorbed in his own happiness, forgetting that of his sister. And soon enough he will undoubtedly learn that the young lady upon whom he has centered his happiness is not all that he believed her to be, and then he will be undone when he considers that he has bartered away the happiness of his sister for a prize that was not worth having. Love, after all, is just a word, Burbage. It has no real meaning—the boy will discover that soon enough."

Burbage paused in his buffing to stare at his master's face. He knew, of course, that Melville was a bitter man and that he intended to have no permanent relationships of his own, but he had never seen him deliberately do such a thing to another.

"But I thought that you liked Landford," he remarked carefully, returning his attention to the boots.

"And I do," replied Melville. "I have shocked you, haven't I, Burbage? Don't you see that this is for his own good? If he learns about the fickleness of love now—that there is no such thing as loyalty and that he cannot rely upon others or even upon his own ability to be constant in love—he will be saved a great deal of misery later."

"And suffer a great deal of misery now, instead," remarked Burbage briefly.

"I see that you disapprove, my friend. Well, I have indeed done the young man a kindness, though he may never thank me for it."

"I doubt he will," agreed the valet, his eyes troubled. "And I had thought, sir," he added slowly, "that you knew that you could rely upon my loyalty."

"I do know that, Burbage," returned Melville, staring at him. "We have been companions since I was a boy. You know that you are the only one in whom I place my trust." And it had been well placed, for one dark night long ago in Portugal, Burbage had risked his own life to carry his wounded master to safety when he could just as easily have left him there and departed with the gold that Melville was carrying—and unlike Melville's mother, Burbage had been told he was remembered in his master's will.

"But according to what you have just said, sir, there will come a day when one of us will break that trust." Burbage stood up stiffly from the kneeling position he had taken to polish the boots. His joints were not as agile as they had once been. "Perhaps I had best let Mae know that I will be joining her soon." His sister ran a small inn in Liverpool, and he planned to retire there when he was too old to serve Melville any longer.

"Nonsense!" replied his master sharply. "What I said has nothing to do with us. Why, we have known one another for almost all of my life!"

"And hasn't Landford known his own sister for that long?" inquired Burbage dryly, pressing his advantage. "If you had had a sister, sir, would you have betrayed her in such a manner?"

"Never!" exclaimed Melville before he could catch himself. "But we will never know that, will we, Burbage?" he added.

Burbage shook his head. "No, sir, but we do know that we have kept our loyalty to one another all these years."

And here he decided he would take advantage of that relationship. "Even though it's not for me to say, sir, it was wrong of you to put the boy in such a position. You may have done more damage than good by playing God."

Melville pondered his valet's words as he made his way to Lady Diana's that morning. He would never allow any human being save Burbage to speak to him in such a manner, but the roots of their relationship went deeply into his childhood. The valet had cared for him since Melville was a very young boy and Burbage a footman in his father's employ. Even though he had done things he knew that Burbage disapproved of, he had never voiced his disagreement so strongly as he had this morning.

To his distress, it was Lady Lavinia who awaited him in the drawing room. "Mr. Melville," she exclaimed warmly, holding out her hands, "I would like to tell you again how much I enjoyed the evening. It was so very kind of you to include me."

"It was my pleasure, ma'am," he assured her, smiling. And it had been, despite the fact that he had been tricked into it. Lady Lavinia, so far as he could tell, was the only individual who deserved no hurt in the business he had undertaken. He had long pitied spinsters who had been obliged to depend upon the generosity of their relatives for their survival, and hearing Diana assure her that she would not be removed from them had troubled him. He had not considered the possibility that his tampering might endanger Lady Lavinia's well-being.

"Mr. Melville," she said slowly, reluctant to enter into the morass that Diana had created, "I am not quite certain how to speak to you about the forthcoming marriage."

"Do you refer to Landford's marriage or to that of the Lady Diana?" he inquired, certain of her answer.

"To Diana's," she replied. "I am afraid that you must have received the wrong impression of what we are like because of that wager."

He watched her intently, curious to see where this was to lead.

Lady Lavinia had taken her handkerchief and was proceeding to wring it between her hands, her rosy cheeks quite pale with the effort she was making. "I

fear that it is all my fault. I have been responsible
for their upbringing, you see, and I have perhaps
been laxer than I should have been with them. I
can see now that their Uncle Robert was right and
more strictness was needed."

"Why do you say so, ma'am?" he inquired easily.

She stared at him, still wringing the small lace
square. "Why, because of what has happened, of
course."

"Nonsense, ma'am!" he replied, determined to
allay her guilt. "Young men will gamble, particularly
when they have first come to town—there is no
shame in that!"

Lady Lavinia trembled involuntarily at the thought
of what he would say if he knew that it had been not
Trevor but Diana doing the gambling. "Yes, perhaps
so," she replied weakly, "but that he should have
made his sister the subject of a wager—"

Since Melville had just been making the same
point himself less than an hour ago, he was hard
pressed to think of a suitable response. "Sometimes,
ma'am," he said finally, "the strain of losing can
rattle one so that it is more difficult to make a decision correctly."

"Yes, I can understand that," said Lady Lavinia
slowly, "but it is still outrageous that Diana should
have been the subject of a wager. If it were known,
she would be ruined."

"I assure you, Lady Lavinia," he said firmly, "that
no one will know of this from me—including her
uncle. I have not the slightest intention of damaging
her good name."

And, somewhat to his own surprise, he knew that

this was true. He intended to teach Landford a lesson, not ruin him or his sister. If he had wished to ruin him, he could have done so quite readily the night of the fateful wager. Having liked the boy, he wanted Landford to learn a lesson that would help him to survive.

Lady Lavinia's eyes had lighted at his words, and she reached out to press his hand warmly. "How very good you are, Mr. Melville!" she exclaimed. "You are far kinder to us than we deserve."

He found it difficult to reply to this, for he knew that he did not merit such praise. In fact, if she knew the truth of the matter, Lady Lavinia would undoubtedly escort him to the front door and see him on his way immediately.

He was saved from replying by the arrival of Diana. "Well, Mr. Melville," she exclaimed lightly as she entered the room, "how kind of you to come to call. I am flattered by your attentiveness. Have you written to Uncle Robert yet?"

Melville, who did not wish to flatter and wished still less to write to Uncle Robert, frowned slightly. "Naturally I have come to pay my respects. As for writing to your uncle, I have not yet done so. I can see no reason to rush."

"Ah, I knew that you were not really interested in marrying me, sir," she sighed, sinking onto the sofa beside the vase of roses. "I fear that I must look elsewhere for a husband."

Lady Lavinia, horrified by her niece's behavior, hurried into speech. "That is no way to speak, Diana. Please forgive her, Mr. Melville," she said, turning to their guest. "You must believe me when I say this is not her normal manner."

Diana fingered the card from Treffington and then tossed it carefully onto the sidetable where Melville would be certain to see it. "But Aunt, how can you expect me to behave normally when I have been rejected?" she asked plaintively. "Clearly Mr. Melville has no desire to marry me, even though he has won the right to do so. I can see that I shall be forced to remain on the shelf all of my days."

Melville had indeed noted the card and the seal, and his color had risen. The chit was a tasteless flirt, willing to associate herself even with such a roué as Treffington, knowing full well from her brother— and from the episode last night—what manner of man he was.

"Undoubtedly you would find Lord Treffington more to your taste, ma'am," he said stiffly, rising as he spoke.

"Treffington!" exclaimed Lady Lavinia, clutching her heart. "Are those roses from him, Diana?"

When her niece nodded, Lady Lavinia sank back among the cushions. "What am I to do with you, Diana? You and Trevor will be the death of me."

Diana hurried to her aunt's side to restore her with her sal volatile, while Melville excused himself and departed with all possible speed. He had not the slightest desire to hear Diana say anything more. Landford, he thought, at least possessed some elegance of mind, but his sister was quite another matter. And the distress that all of this had brought to Lady Lavinia was more than he wanted to think about at the moment. Seldom in his life had Melville felt the twinges of guilt. Perhaps, he reflected, a few hours at his club would restore some peace of mind.

In the meantime, Diana had managed to restore her aunt just before the arrival of Trevor and Tom. However, before they could be informed of what had transpired to overset Lady Lavinia, the butler opened the door to announce yet another guest.

"Mr. Robert Barton," he said briefly, standing aside so that gentleman could enter. All four of the occupants of the drawing room stared up in dismay at the man standing there. It was indeed Uncle Robert.

Thirteen

"Why, what a surprise, Mr. Barton," said Lady Lavinia feebly, rising from the sofa and extending her hand. "We had no idea you were coming."

"Of course you did not," he announced, looking them over distastefully. Diana had often remarked that Uncle Robert always looked as though he had just eaten something that disagreed with him. "You did not think that I was aware you were in London, but I am kept better informed than that. I knew almost immediately that you had come to town without my permission."

"I should have suspected that you would have an informer in the neighborhood at home," said Diana bitterly, wondering which of the people in the village was the spy. "I hope that you did not have to pay too dearly for the information, Uncle."

He glared at her a moment, then sat down rather heavily. "I should not have to pay for such information. One would think that my own family members would remember their obligations—and that you, Lady Lavinia, as their guardian, would certainly remember yours," he returned gravely.

"Oh, do leave Aunt Lavinia alone, Uncle. Your

quarrel is with me, not with her!" exclaimed Diana impatiently.

"I will come to you soon enough, Missy," he assured her, ignoring the effect of that name upon her as he turned toward her brother. "My first quarrel is with you, sir—although I did not realize it until I reached London last night."

"And what is the nature of that quarrel, Uncle Robert?" Trevor asked, knowing full well what he was about to hear.

"It has come to my attention that you think yourself engaged," said his uncle, speaking as though Trevor had just been taken before the magistrate for highway robbery.

"I don't 'think' myself engaged, Uncle—I am indeed engaged," returned Trevor proudly, standing a little taller. "I am engaged to Lady Genevieve Linden."

Robert Barton waved his hand in a gesture of dismissal. "Yes, I know that you have attempted to attach yourself to Appelby's girl. I might have known that you would make such a choice if left to your own devices."

Trevor's face darkened. "What do you mean by that remark, sir?" he demanded. "If you have anything disrespectful to say about her, I shall be forced to—to—" He searched for words, but they failed him.

"To do what, Trevor?" asked his uncle dryly. "To call me out?"

"No, of course not, but—"

"Young man, you are underage and you know that

you must have my permission to marry," said Mr. Barton.

"Yes, I am aware of that," admitted Trevor.

"Then why did you not come to me and ask me for permission?"

Trevor, unwilling to disclose the problem with Treffington, simply said, "There was no time, sir. It simply happened."

Mr. Barton snorted. "Well, it will simply 'unhappen,' " he returned. "I do not give my permission for so ill-considered an alliance. I am grateful that there has been no formal announcement of it."

Trevor stared at him. "You cannot mean, Uncle, that you expect me to cry off," he said in disbelief.

"You will not be crying off. There is no statement to withdraw," said his uncle. "Since there has been no formal announcement, this will pass quickly."

"There is an understanding between myself and Lady Genevieve and between me and her father," returned Trevor. "I will not break faith with either of them."

"You have no choice." His uncle stared at him coldly. "How will you support her if you have no income?"

"This is all very easy for you to say, sir, since you have no real knowledge of me nor of the situation, and you have no interest in gaining that knowledge. If I were of age, I would marry her immediately, despite anything that you might say!"

"When you are of age, you may go to the devil in whatever manner pleases you!" retorted his uncle. "At the moment, however, your welfare is my business, and I will not give my consent!"

"And what if I marry in spite of that?" demanded Trevor. "What will you do then?"

"I shall cut off your allowance," he replied.

"Do you have the power to do that?" asked Diana sharply. "I thought that the matter of our quarterly allowance was set in the terms of our father's will."

Mr. Barton glowered at her, for he was aware that her observation was accurate. Diana sat back in satisfaction, pleased that she had for the moment discomfited him.

"I will deal with you shortly, Missy!" he exclaimed as he rose indignantly. "You had no business coming here without my permission, as you and your aunt very well know."

He glared at them all for a moment. "I have made a long and tiring trip in a very short time, and I am going to repair to my club to rest. In the meantime, I forbid you, Diana, to set foot out of this house!"

Before she could retort, he focused on Trevor. "And you, young man, keep your distance from Appelby's girl and do nothing to fan the flame of this engagement nonsense!"

And he turned and stalked from the room before either of them could reply.

"Well, I'll do no such thing as sit within this house simply because he has said to do so!" exclaimed Diana as the door shut behind him. "It would not matter if it were pouring buckets, I should go out immediately!"

"Nor will I stay away from Jenny!" said her brother, pacing up and down the room in agitation. "Of all the high and mighty—just who does he think he is?"

"Your guardian," replied Lady Lavinia feebly, lifting her vinaigrette to her nose once more. She was beginning to feel that she was really too old for all of this.

"What will you do, Trev?" asked Tom bleakly. "He holds the purse strings."

"Don't I know it? The old miser! One would think it was his own money instead of mine!" Trevor continued to pace, running his hands through his hair until it stood in dark spikes while the others sat in glum silence.

Finally he collapsed onto the sofa and dropped his head into his hands. "What shall we do, Di?" he asked brokenly. "My allowance isn't enough for us to get by on, and if we wait, Appelby will be back in the basket within the month and I'll have nothing with which to bail him out. As sure as fire, he'll hand Jenny off to Treffington or whoever else is the highest bidder! How am I to bear this? How can I possibly explain it to her?"

"You won't have to," said his sister firmly, sitting bolt upright in her chair.

The other three turned to stare at her.

"Why not, Di?" asked Tom apprehensively. "Why won't Trev have to tell her? What can we possibly do to prevent it?"

Diana smiled purposefully and Tom felt his heart sink. "I shall marry, of course," she returned. "After all, I must marry sometime, and it might as well be now if it will save Trevor's happiness."

"What are you talking about?" demanded her brother.

"All right," said Tom in a small voice, preparing

himself for the moment of sacrifice. "Would you do
me the honor of becoming my wife, Di?"

Diana stared at him for a moment. "Tom, have
you been into the brandy?" she inquired, laughing.
Then, seeing his bewildered expression, she leaned
over and kissed him on the cheek. "It's very dear
of you, Tom," she said gently, "but I'm not trying
to make you marry me."

"I should be honored if you would accept my offer," said Tom, his voice growing stronger. After all,
he told himself, one must take care of one's friends.

"Nonsense, Tom," replied Diana. "You know the
provisions made for you. Even if you did marry me,
we would have only our joint allowances until we
both come of age. We would be no better off, nor
would we be able to help Trevor."

Her brother shook his head. "What are you talking about, Di?" he demanded. "Of course you're
not going to marry Tom! What in heaven's name
are you rattling on about?"

"I am not rattling, Trevor. I shall force Melville
to marry me," she said briefly. "Once I have, I shall
force him to provide support for you and Jenny until
you are of age."

"You must be mad!" exclaimed Trevor. "The only
reason I haven't called him out is because you said
that this was all a hoax and there would be no need
for you to marry him—that he had no desire to do
so."

"Well, the case has changed now," observed his
sister, "and it really is of little consequence whether
he wishes to marry me. It is now a necessity."

She moved close to him and put her arm around

his waist. "After all, Trev, we have always known that most women make marriages of convenience— Jenny is one of the lucky ones who will be able to marry for love—so why should I not marry someone at a time that will benefit you?"

She did not add that she did not think that she would particularly mind the match herself, that she found Melville quite appealing, in fact. Trevor would never believe her, or—if he did—he would be appalled.

"You will do no such thing, Di," he said firmly, rising and smoothing his hair. "I shall have to think of something—though heaven only knows what it will be. Come along, Tom," he said briefly, stopping only to kiss their aunt on the cheek as he left. "I daresay if I leave you, you will try to force Di to marry you."

Bending over Lady Lavinia, he hugged her tightly. "Don't worry, Aunt," he said. "We will come about all right."

"Indeed we will," murmured his sister as he left, "indeed we will."

Poor Lady Lavinia took to her bed with a ferocious headache, cautioning her niece to do no more than take a brief walk for a breath of fresh air. "Your uncle means what he says, my dear," she said, tearfully kissing Diana. "Pray don't antagonize him anymore than we already have. Once he learns that Trevor paid Lord Appelby, it will all be over for us."

"I shall take care of things, Aunt," Diana reassured her. "Pray do not worry." And, once certain that poor Lady Lavinia was abed and asleep, she sat down to plan her course.

She had, of course, not the slightest intention of remaining indoors, confined to quarters as her uncle had indicated, nor would she allow him to send her home. She was well aware that her parents would have had her coming-out several years ago had they lived, and she felt well within her rights to attend what parties she wished, even though she had not been formally presented. As Landford's sister, she could expect to be invited everywhere. And as her thoughts took this turn, she remembered Lady Rigsby.

Resolutely she went upstairs and dressed herself to call upon that lady, a good friend of her mother's, who had remained in desultory contact with Diana over the years, always offering her services should Diana decide that she would like to be formally presented at court. She had been away from London two years ago, the last time that Diana and Lady Lavinia visited the city.

Diana had planned to go and visit that lady once they settled themselves in London this time, but her plans had, of course, gone badly awry when she arrived to discover Trevor's difficulty. Now, however, she felt that she could use Lady Rigsby's help to overset any plans her uncle might have for returning her to the country.

"You poor child!" exclaimed Lady Rigsby, who was delighted to have Diana arrive at her home, no matter how early, and who was appalled to hear of her uncle's high-handed treatment.

After presenting her card to the butler, Diana had been escorted immediately to that lady's boudoir, where Lady Rigsby smothered her in a flowery embrace. "Your mother was such a dear, dear woman—whatever possessed her to leave you in the clutches of such a beastly man?"

She listened in rapt silence while Diana recounted her tale of woe—a carefully edited tale, of course.

"Well," Diana temporized, "Uncle Robert is an excellent steward of our estate, of course, but Aunt Lavinia—my father's sister—is the one who has reared us."

"Dear Lavinia!" exclaimed Lady Rigsby. "I have not seen her since—well, since she broke her engagement to Robert Locksley and retired to the country."

"Aunt Lavinia was engaged?" asked Diana in disbelief. "I had not realized that she had ever had an attachment of any sort."

"Oh, yes, my dear—oh yes, indeed!" exclaimed Lady Rigsby, drawing her chair closer. "It was quite the talk of the *ton* when it happened, you know. Locksley had never looked twice at any woman until Lavinia came to town, and then—well, he was completely overset by her. They were engaged within a month of her being presented. No one could believe it because he was quite a catch, my dear."

"But what happened?" demanded Diana. "Why did they not marry? Why did Aunt Lavinia leave London?"

Lady Rigsby shrugged, her bright blue eyes wide. "That is why it was a nine-day wonder," she explained. "No one knew what happened. In fact, so far as I know, no one ever knew."

Diana sat silently for a few moments, sipping the chocolate that Lady Rigsby had pressed upon her.

A nine-day wonder indeed. Why had her aunt never mentioned this? For the moment, Diana quite forgot her present problems. Why had her aunt, that most sociable of all souls, never mentioned any of this to her?

"But, my dear," said Lady Rigsby, bringing her back to earth, "tell me more about your dilemma. Why ever would your uncle be ordering you back to the country when you are already past the age for presentation? Does the man wish for you to die a spinster?"

"A very good question, Lady Rigsby," Diana agreed. "Actually, I believe that he thinks that life in London is unsuited for a young lady and that I should be better off to live a secluded life in the country, doing good works."

"A Methodist!" exclaimed that lady in horror, clapping her hands to her cheeks. "But I cannot believe that he would inflict his beliefs upon you when your father and mother were so very much a part of this society! How could he justify separating you from it?"

"Perhaps because he feels that my mother would still be alive had she not come here with my father," replied Diana.

"What nonsense!" exclaimed Lady Rigsby sharply. "Your parents were very happy together, Diana, and the accident that befell them could have occurred anywhere. Your uncle is nonsensical to believe otherwise."

"Unfortunately, he is accustomed to listening to no one save himself," observed Diana.

"Well, he shall have to hear from someone else

on this matter. Your mother and I had talked about it," said Lady Rigsby sharply, rising and ringing for her maid. When that young woman entered, she said, "I am about to go out, Marie. We must hurry. And send Baker to tell his master that I must see him before he goes out today."

Diana stared at her. "Do you mean that you are going to see him now, ma'am?" she asked blankly.

"I am going to send my husband to see him first," said Lady Rigsby crisply, "since ladies are not allowed at the clubs. You must write down his direction for me, and Lord Rigsby shall go round to see him immediately; then I shall meet them for luncheon. My husband is fully capable of setting your uncle in motion."

Diana watched in amazement as she bustled about, making her arrangements, and by the time she left, she had no doubt that Lady Rigsby would do precisely what she said she would do. Diana could almost find it in her heart to pity her uncle—but not quite.

"You go home and tell dear Lavinia that I shall come to see her as soon as possible," Lady Rigsby informed her, "and the two of you need to see to your wardrobes, for you are about to attend as many routs as it is possible to fit into a day."

Happily, Diana did precisely as she was told, and she was delighted to see that her aunt also brightened when she shared the news with her.

"Sally Rigsby?" she said in disbelief. "Why, I haven't seen her since—I haven't seen her in years!"

Diana watched her aunt gravely. "Lady Rigsby told me about Robert Locksley, Aunt," she said slowly, uncertain whether or not she should mention it. Since she had always been perfectly honest with Lady Lavinia, she decided that she should not be otherwise now. Still, she was unhappy to see her aunt flush painfully.

"That was a good many years ago, my dear—too many to bother about," she said.

"But not so many that you've forgotten him, Aunt," Diana observed. "You have turned a brilliant pink, and that is not on my account, I know."

They sat in silence for a few minutes, then Diana took Lady Lavinia's plump little hand. "Tell me about him, Aunt," she said gently. "Who is this Robert Locksley? Some handsome young man who broke your heart years ago?"

Lady Lavinia shook her head. "He didn't break my heart. He was a handsome man, surely enough, but older than I was then, and I thought that a problem—the more fool I!"

"Do you mean he offered for you and you broke the engagement because you thought him too old?" asked Diana in disbelief.

Her aunt nodded, her normally cheerful expression clouded with regret. "Well, it wasn't all just because of his age. I was just a foolish girl then," she said, "but that does not excuse it. I loved him, but I was an innocent and I discovered that, although he had not married, he had had numerous relationships with other women."

"Do you mean 'prime articles,' as Trevor would say, Aunt?" inquired Diana curiously.

"Honestly, Diana!" exclaimed Lady Lavinia. "You

should not say such things—nor even know about them! Your Uncle Robert—"

"Never mind Uncle Robert," returned Diana unpenitently. "And if you had known about such things, you probably would not have reacted as you did."

"Perhaps," sighed her aunt. "At any rate, I ran away to the country and convinced myself that he was far too old for me and that I had made a wise decision."

"How much older was he?" inquired Diana.

"Ten years," replied Lady Lavinia. "But at the time I felt that it might as well be fifty. That shows just how young I was at the time."

"Well, Aunt," Diana said thoughtfully, "ten years does seem quite a bit older, I must confess."

"Mr. Melville is ten years older than you are, my dear," observed Lady Lavinia. "Does he seem too old to be interesting?" She watched her niece with interest, for she had not been hoodwinked by Diana's pretense of sacrificing herself for her brother.

Diana thought for a moment of Melville's intense green eyes and his dark face. "No," she said slowly, "when you put it so, ten years does not seem so very much older."

"Then you are wiser than I was," murmured her aunt. "Although, to be sure, I was only seventeen at the time and scarcely out of the schoolroom. Still, I should have had more sense, but I told poor Robert he was too old for me."

"And you never mentioned the other women?"

"Naturally not," said Lavinia. "It wouldn't have been suitable."

"But why did you leave London?" asked Diana.

"Because I didn't want to talk to anyone about the other women and because I was ashamed to be thought a jilt," returned Lady Lavinia. "I thought that I would be ridiculed, so I went home to wait until people had forgotten all about it."

"And he went away, too?" asked Diana sadly.

Lady Lavinia nodded slowly. "Yes, he did," she replied. "He went back to his country estates, and I went back to Leamington to recover from the disgrace of being a jilt.

"What a fool I was," she said, shaking her head. "By the time I had decided that I had made a mistake, it was too late."

"Why was it too late? Had he married someone else?"

Lady Lavinia shook her head. "He went out to Barbados to look after his family plantation there— just to get away, I know." Here she stopped and stared out the window.

"Well, and what happened?" asked Diana. "What happened when he came home?"

"Robert never came home," she replied simply. "He caught a fever there and died. It was when I heard that I knew I had made a mistake."

"And he died without knowing that you cared anything for him," remarked Diana sadly. "How very unhappy you must have been."

Lady Lavinia nodded again. "I thought so many times of writing to him," she said, "but pride would not allow me to do so. After all," she smiled a little painfully, "what was I to say? No one else of interest offered for me, and how would it have looked for me to write to him that I had made a mistake when I had been left on the shelf?"

Diana hugged her aunt violently. "On the shelf? How can you say such a thing, Aunt? You know that you could have had anyone you wished to have! Why, you have had at least three offers I know of since I was old enough to notice that sort of thing!"

Her aunt smiled a little waterily, wiping her eyes.

"You know that is so!" Diana reminded her. "And I know that you would not entertain any of them because of Trevor and me—you had us to care for!"

"Don't be a goose, my dear," said Lavinia. "I made no sacrifices for you and Trevor. No one who offered for me ever tempted me. Robert is the only one who ever meant anything to me. And I sent him away and he died, so I grew old alone." She paused for a moment, thinking. "No, of course that isn't true," she amended. "I have you and Trevor."

Diana sat thoughtfully, her cheek against Lavinia's cheek, patting her aunt's gray curls. Stories should have happier endings than Lady Lavinia's had, she thought. And there would be for Trevor and Jenny, she thought, feeling a rush of determination. There was no need for them to be made unhappy.

"Lady Rigsby has sent her husband to speak with Uncle Robert," remarked Diana, eager to take her aunt's mind off her unhappy love affair. "Can you imagine what he will think when he is approached in the privacy of his club? He will be madder than fire."

This sally had the hoped-for effect. Her aunt laughed heartily, wiping her eyes after a few moments. "I fear that Mr. Barton has met his match," she remarked cheerfully, sounding like herself again. "Sally has no fear in her heart. He may as well give up the struggle now."

"I would give a monkey to see his face when Lord Rigsby descends upon him and informs him that he is to dine with Lady Rigsby and discuss my coming-out."

Lady Lavinia wiped her eyes with her wisp of lace. "I would feel sorry for Robert Barton if he hadn't spent his life dealing us so much misery. As it is, I can only be grateful that Sally is on our side."

"I should say so!" exclaimed Diana with feeling. "I should hate to think that she was ranged on the other side."

Lady Lavinia caught up Diana's hand and held it to her own cheek, studying her intently. "My dear, marriage is a serious matter. I know that you would do anything for Trevor, but marrying a man who won your hand in a card game is too much to ask."

"No one is asking that of me, Aunt," replied Diana calmly. "You know that what I said about marriage for us is true. It is a matter of the greatest luck if a marriage is a love match. In fact, being in love with your mate is almost regarded as poor taste among the *ton*. You know that."

Lavinia nodded. "Still, what do you really know of Mr. Melville, Diana?" she asked. "I could not bear it if you were unhappy in your marriage. There would be nothing that either Trevor or I could do to help you, you know. You would have stepped beyond our reach. Everything you own and are would become his."

For a moment Diana felt the shadow of her aunt's fear pass over her, but she brushed it aside. "Just think of it, Aunt. You know that you find him charming—do you not?"

Lady Lavinia nodded, dimpling. "He is a very taking man," she admitted. "But that does not mean that he will make a good husband, my dear." She hesitated a moment. "Some men are short-tempered, you know, and are not above striking their wives—and, after all, the wife is the property of the husband."

"And do you think Mr. Melville is such a man, Aunt?" she asked.

Lavinia shook her head. "He does not appear to be so, but appearances can be quite distressingly deceiving, Diana. I should hate to find out that my judgment of him was wrong when you will be the one to pay the price."

Diana laughed. "Do you think that I cannot hold my own?" she inquired merrily. "After all, think of Lady Rigsby. Does she seem to be poorly used by her husband?"

Her aunt allowed herself to be cheered by the raillery. "Yes, I know what you are capable of, my dear," she admitted. "And I do believe that Mr. Melville is a very taking gentleman."

"I declare, Aunt, I think I should be quite jealous. You think so highly of that gentleman, and I know that he is uncommonly fond of you!"

"Nonsense!" exclaimed Lavinia, blushing and laughing.

Content with her work, Diana teased her aunt un-
mercifully for the next few minutes, effectively ban-
ishing her fears and misgivings—for the moment, at
any rate.

Fourteen

Precisely what the details of the first meeting between Lady Rigsby and Uncle Robert were went unrecorded, but Diana and Lady Lavinia were not long left in doubt as to the impact of that meeting. A messenger arrived from Uncle Robert's club in the afternoon, informing them that they would be attending the theatre that evening in the company of Lord and Lady Rigsby.

"Well, Aunt," she announced gleefully, "I see that you did not underrate your friend's powers. We have Uncle Robert at bay."

"For the moment," agreed Lavinia, a little mournfully. "I cannot help but believe that we shall pay dearly for this in the long run, however."

Diana, not being particularly concerned about the long run and concentrating entirely on an enjoyable evening, sent a note to Trevor to tell him the good news and to assure him that she was putting her plan into effect immediately.

Accordingly, she wrote another note to Jack Melville, informing him where she would be that evening and inviting him to stop by the Rigsbys' box if he should be in attendance. "Not," she added to the note, "that you should do so if you have no desire to come—for heaven knows I would not and could not compel you to do so—but I do so look forward to some time spent with a gentleman of discretion. I understand that Lord Treffington will be present, so your company too would be most welcome."

Diana smiled as she sealed the note. Doubtless Melville had no desire whatsoever to attend the theatre that evening. And doubtless he cared still less to spend time catering to her. Nonetheless, she was quite certain that the mention of Treffington would bring Melville to heel. He had seen the roses and the note that morning, and he would understand her allusion. She suspected strongly that, although he had no genuine desire to marry her, he still considered her his property, fairly won, and she knew that he was interested in Trevor's reaction to the situation. And, thinking of the interlude in the garden at Lady Sotheby's, she knew that the attraction between them was strong. All in all, she was certain he would come.

"Treffington!" exclaimed Melville, finishing her note and tossing it to the floor in irritation. "What can she possibly mean by having any sort of contact with such a man as that?" he demanded of Burbage. "She knows full well what manner of man he is, for her brother has told her about Treffington's plan for marrying Lady Genevieve!"

"Possibly, sir," observed Burbage quietly, picking up the note and placing it upon his master's desk, "the young lady would wish to draw to your attention the possibility that she might spend time with that gentleman if you do not present yourself."

"Blackmail!" seethed Melville. "It is no more than blackmail, Burbage! How can you possibly countenance such behavior?"

The valet shrugged gently. "She is not blackmailing me, sir, so you see that I tend to look upon it more lightly than I might otherwise."

Melville laughed reluctantly and crushed the note. "A very good point," he admitted. "And I'm afraid that she does have my attention. I would prefer that she not allow herself to be in close contact with such a man as Treffington. And I am certain that she knows as much and is using that to her own advantage."

Burbage studied his master. Melville had shown small regard for the well-being of ladies he had had contact with in the past—this, in fact, appeared to be a first. Why he would worry about Lady Diana being seen with such a man as Treffington was beyond the valet's ken, given the uncomplimentary things he had said about her. Certainly he had shown a partiality for Lord Landford that was most unusual, but to extend it to that gentleman's sister was reaching far beyond what Burbage had known as his master's typical behavior.

"And Lord Landford, sir," he inquired diffidently, "do you see much of him these days?"

Melville shook his head impatiently. "Little enough—and what little I see is probably too much."

Burbage looked at him in surprise. "Forgive me,

sir, but I had thought that you found him a most enjoyable young man," he ventured.

Melville nodded. "And so I did. But now—well, now Landford is fully absorbed in his Lady Genevieve and has no time for anyone or anything else."

"Surely that is natural," said Burbage, still watching Melville carefully. "One would expect a young man to be most attentive to the lady of his choice."

"Well of course you would!" exclaimed his master impatiently. "That's not the point at all, Burbage."

His valet looked at him expectantly, having not the least notion what the point was.

"Well, actually, Burbage," Melville admitted slowly, "I find Landford quite dull these days, and I can't think why I was ever interested in him at all."

"Then why are you still spending your time with him?" asked Burbage in genuine wonder. If ever there was someone who did not suffer fools gladly, his master was that one.

Melville looked uncomfortable. "Lady Lavinia, of course, is a charming and devoted aunt."

Burbage nodded. "You have said as much, sir. And so you are spending time with them because you are quite smitten by the aunt?"

Melville shook his head impatiently. "Don't make me sound a fool, Burbage! Of course I am doing no such thing. I am interested in—well, I am interested in Lady Diana!"

He paused, somewhat startled by his own words. It was true, however. He had not felt that way at first, but now it seemed to him that her conversation was often quick and lively—even if often at his expense. And, should he wish to put an end to matters, he knew that he only had to go to her uncle and ask for her hand, for that gentleman would undoubtedly refuse him upon the basis of his reputation.

Burbage looked at him in wonder. Melville had admitted interest in no female for years. "I had not realized that you had changed your view of her," he said slowly. "I knew, naturally, that there was something there that drew you back again and again, but I confess that I thought it was the young lady's brother."

"That's what the young lady thinks, too," said Melville quietly, "which is all very well. This is a most curious situation I find myself in, and I confess that I have not been able to make out her character as clearly as I had at first thought I could."

"Indeed?" inquired Burbage thoughtfully. "You have said that she is high-handed, I believe," he observed after a few moments of silence.

Melville nodded. "She is most definitely that." He paused and considered the matter for a moment or two. "And I thought at first that she possessed no delicacy of mind when she was not shocked by the news that her brother had wagered her in a card game."

"But now?" asked Burbage, when no further observation was forthcoming.

Melville shook his head. "That's just it, Burbage. I have no idea. She appears to be trying to force me to marry her, although I feel quite certain that she has no wish to marry me."

"Perhaps it is for her brother's sake," ventured Burbage.

Melville shrugged. "Perhaps. But I see no reason for it. After all, Landford will marry his ladylove, apparently without any significant qualms of conscience about his sister. He gave the money to Appelby and the wedding will be soon, I should imagine. So why would she bother to antagonize me by seeing Treffington?"

Burbage, quite naturally, had no suitable response for this, but he watched with some satisfaction as his master prepared to go to the theatre that evening. At the very least, this young lady and her brother had stirred more emotion in Melville than he had shown in many months.

And, to do her justice, Diana had every intention of stirring even more emotion than she had. Although he made her blood run cold, she forced herself to flirt with Treffington in their box that evening, watching over her fan for any sign of the recalcitrant Melville. When at last he put in an appearance, she was relieved to see that Treffington removed himself immediately, not being particularly interested in jeopardizing his health.

After greeting Lady Lavinia and Lord and Lady Rigsby, he whispered to Diana as he settled himself next to her. "Your taste in company is still impeccable, I see."

She smiled blandly. "Why, Mr. Melville," she drawled, "I did not realize that you were a vain man."

"I believe you know quite well to whom I refer," he responded, unruffled by this sally.

"Dear Treffington?" she inquired. "He appears to be so interested in making my stay in London an enjoyable one. I am quite overcome by his kind attentions."

"And just what attentions would those be?" he asked, his voice growing sharper.

Pleased with his reaction, she said sweetly, "Why, he has offered to take me riding in the park tomorrow, and to escort me to Vauxhall in the evening."

"Now there that would be a pretty picture," he murmured. "An old profligate like Treffington taking you unescorted to such a place as Vauxhall. I do, naturally, forbid you to do any such thing."

"Do you indeed?" she replied, her voice still honeyed. "And precisely what right do you have to forbid me to do anything I should wish to do?"

"If your own common sense does not rule here, surely that of your brother will," he responded, his tone drawing the attention of the others in the box even though he kept his voice low.

Flushing slightly, he bowed to Lady Lavinia. "I am afraid that your niece and I were disagreeing over the lines of one of the actors."

Lady Rigsby regarded him with some astonishment. "Indeed? Why, I had no idea that you were so taken with the theatre, Melville. Indeed, I cannot recall having seen you here save once or twice before."

He again bowed but had recovered his equanimity. "I believe that you will find, Lady Rigsby, that there are many things you do not know about me."

Lady Rigsby laughed and tapped him on the shoulder with her fan. "I have always found you interesting, Melville," she conceded, "and now I discover that you are amusing as well."

"I had not realized that you were at all acquainted with the Rigsbys," murmured Diana as he once more seated himself close to her.

"I might be making the same observation, ma'am—and with more justification, since you are the one who has made your home in the country."

"She was a friend of my mother's," she replied, "and she is acquainted with my aunt as well."

"I see." He did not speak for a few minutes, apparently absorbed by what was taking place on the stage, although Diana was certain his mind was elsewhere. "Perhaps Lady Rigsby will be able to persuade you to see that allowing Treffington to dance attendance upon you is a mistake. Or perhaps your brother can convince you of that."

"I notice, Mr. Melville, that you are no longer forbidding me to do so yourself," she observed, casting him a sidelong glance. "Does that mean that you do not care about the behavior of your future wife—or that you no longer consider me your future wife?"

He turned to look at her squarely, his eyebrows disdainfully arched. "Have you no delicacy of mind at all, ma'am?" he asked coldly.

Diana considered his question for a moment, then shook her head. "I cannot see that delicacy of mind is an option for someone whose future has been the subject of a wager."

"And does Lady Rigsby know of the wager?" he asked abruptly, his voice still low.

"Of course not," she returned. "It is scarcely news

that I would share with anyone who had no need of knowing it. And I most certainly did not tell Uncle Robert when he arrived."

There was another perceptible pause in the conversation while he took in what she had said. "Your uncle is in town, then?" he asked.

Diana nodded, noting with satisfaction that his expression appeared to have frozen for a moment.

"Why is he not here with you this evening?" he inquired. "One would think he would wish to spend time with you and your aunt."

"I've told you about Uncle Robert," she said briefly. "He only comes to order us about, not to spend time with us. His life lies in managing his investments. Should you wish to see him, you would have to make an appointment with him."

"Indeed?" said Melville, considering the matter carefully. He had not the slightest intention of having her force his hand. "Is that what you must do yourself, then? Make an appointment?"

She nodded. "Only I do not do so, naturally. I have not the slightest wish to speak with him, and when he feels he must speak with us, he does so." She stopped a moment, remembering with pleasure Lady Rigsby's triumphant invasion upon her uncle's time, and smiled.

"And what is it that you find amusing about that?" asked Melville curiously.

"Merely that Lady Rigsby had her husband beard the lion in his den today. Lord Rigsby took my uncle by surprise at his club and carried him away to speak with Lady Rigsby about my having a season since I have never had anything more than casual visits here with Aunt Lavinia and Trevor. She told him that I must be presented at court and that she was arranging it."

Melville smiled appreciatively. "And I take it that your uncle would not enjoy hearing that."

Diana chuckled. "Scarcely. It must have been a double blow to him—being ordered about by a mere female and having to allow me to become a part of the decadent life of London society."

"And so why would he give way to her since he is your guardian? Would his not be the final decision?"

She shrugged. "Lady Rigsby pointed out to him that he had an obligation to my parents to see me married well." She glanced at him. "She could not know, of course, that I am, in a manner of speaking, already engaged."

It was Melville's turn to shrug. "Do not allow me to stand in your way," he observed coolly. "It would be to my benefit to take a wife who has been properly introduced to society. Do as you will—for the moment."

He stood and looked down at her for a moment, then leaned down and whispered, "Except that I forbid you to spend your time with Treffington."

Diana stiffened, but managed a noncommittal smile as he bid the others a good evening and departed.

"Really, Diana!" observed Lady Rigsby crossly. "I know that your upbringing has not been a traditional one and that you are no schoolroom miss, but how on earth did you acquire two such infamous

admirers as Treffington and Melville—and in so
short a time?"

Lady Lavinia paled, but her friend was fully occupied with her charge, Lord Rigsby having left the
box to meet some friends in the lobby.

"Are they so very dreadful?" inquired Diana in-
nocently. "I met Lord Treffington at Lady Sotheby's
evening party last night, and he has been most attentive."

"I daresay," replied Lady Rigsby dryly, "one could
say the same thing of a leech—and they are equally
attractive."

Diana laughed. "Well, I do admit that I do not
find him excessively attractive."

"I am reassured," replied the lady. "Melville, however, is quite another case, and he *is* excessively attractive—and excessively dangerous."

"Is he, indeed?" inquired Diana, widening her
eyes. "In what way dangerous, Lady Rigsby?"

"You know very well, my dear," returned her
new friend. "I was watching the two of you, and
he is far too familiar in his manner with you. How
came you to know him?"

Diana saw her aunt sit up straighter and her hand
go instinctively to her reticule for her vinaigrette.
"He is an acquaintance of Trevor's, Lady Rigsby, and
he has been kind enough to call upon us." From
the corner of her eye, she saw Lady Lavinia replace
the vinaigrette in her reticule and lean back in her
chair in relief.

"Judging by Melville's manner with you, he appears to have moved beyond the stage of being an

acquaintance," remarked Lady Rigsby. "You really should not encourage him, you know."

"Why should I not?" Diana inquired. "You appeared to get on well enough with him. And he certainly is much more personable than Treffington."

"That is precisely the danger, my dear. He is much too personable. As an old married lady, I have some degree of safety from wagging tongues, but for a man like Melville to pay such particular attentions on a young woman just come to town—" She paused and shrugged. "It would cause unpleasant talk, I fear."

Diana's shoulders straightened. "And should I fear being talked about, ma'am?" she asked bluntly.

Lady Rigsby nodded seriously. "Indeed you should. Until you are safely engaged, your reputation must remain impeccable. Otherwise, you may frighten off possible suitors."

"I would not want a man who could be frightened away," remarked Diana.

"That's all very well to say now," returned Lady Rigsby practically. "But should you find yourself without a suitable young man because of your behavior, you might feel very differently."

Although she disagreed violently, Diana caught her aunt's warning eye and managed to check her retort. After all, she had no wish to alienate Lady Rigsby, who was going to considerable trouble on her behalf.

She smiled at Lady Lavinia reassuringly. She had every intention of enjoying herself and of pressing Melville into marriage before he knew what she was about.

Her quarry, on the other hand, told himself that he needed to remain as close as possible to Landford and his sister in order to see the outcome of the "lesson" he was teaching and to be amused by Lady Diana's machinations. He had decided that his wager had been well worth the money, for he had been badly in need of a diversion. Life had grown far too boring before the advent of the Ballingers.

Fifteen

Thanks to Lady Rigsby, life for Lady Diana and her aunt became a whirl of activities. Uncle Robert had put in one morose appearance in the four days since his arrival, but since it had been brief and he was not denying them their new-found social life, Diana was unperturbed. He had not weakened his stance about Trevor's engagement, however, and refused roundly when Trevor asked to bring Jenny to meet him, certain that she would make a favorable impression.

"Never mind, Trevor," Diana reassured him after this encounter. "We shall come about. Leave this to me."

"That's all very well to say, Di," he returned, ruffling his hair in despair once more, "but I won't have you hatching another crackbrained scheme that could land us farther in the basket than we already are."

"If I hadn't hatched that first 'crackbrained scheme,' as you call it, Jenny would already be married to Treffington," Diana reminded him tartly.

"I know, I know," he groaned. "Never mind what I say, Di. I know that you did what you thought was best, but it'll do us no good now. Treffington has already put in another appearance. He came to call on Jenny yesterday and brought her a huge bouquet of roses. Just like those," he added, pointing to her arrangement on a table in the corner of the drawing room.

"He didn't!" exclaimed Diana. "Why, the Friday-faced old—"

"Diana!" exclaimed Lady Lavinia, entering the room in time to hear her response.

"It's Treffington, Aunt!" she returned. "He's come back to bother Jenny."

"Oh, no," replied Lady Lavinia, seating herself beside Trevor and taking his hand. "I am so very sorry, my dear."

"It's only to be expected," he sighed. "I haven't yet told Appleby about Uncle Robert's decision, but he has been asking when he can send the announcement of our engagement to the paper, and I have been putting him off. I daresay that he is beginning to realize that it isn't going to happen."

"But he has his money," Diana pointed out practically.

"Yes, and as we know, that will last him no longer than an April snow," he responded dismally.

It was this conversation that sent Diana into battle at full tilt. She and Trevor attended a ball that evening, a crush at which she had every expectation of encountering Melville. He had been quite faithful in his attentions to her since the wager. Lady Rigsby remarked upon the surprise of seeing him so frequently at social events he had never frequented before, eying Diana warningly as she did so.

"Why should he not come?" inquired Diana carelessly, raising one white shoulder in a shrug as she adjusted the flowers in the bodice of her gown before going into the ball that evening.

"Why should he come now when he has seldom done so before? That is the question to be asked," replied Lady Rigsby tartly. "And I believe that we know the answer to that, my dear. He is quite attentive to you."

Diana considered this remark with satisfaction. He had indeed been most attentive, dancing with her more than the two dances considered acceptable, talking with her, standing near her when she was talking with others. And always, she thought, he watched her. Even when he appeared to be looking elsewhere, she was keenly aware that he was focused upon her. It gave her a gratifying sense of power. And, she thought, it was time to use that power. Trevor's affairs were becoming increasingly serious.

Accordingly, at the ball that evening, she raised her eyes to Melville's during a waltz and smiled invitingly. "I am feeling a trifle warm, sir," she said. "Perhaps it would be wise to find a place where we could enjoy a breath of fresh air. There is far too great a crush of people here tonight."

"There is indeed," he replied thoughtfully, wondering why she was suddenly behaving in such a forward manner.

For the past few days she had flaunted her newfound popularity in his face as he watched her dance with her new admirers. He sat amidst the throng of new visitors in her drawing room, chatting more often with Lady Lavinia than with Diana. He had not been unduly troubled by all of this, for it had been amusing to watch her at play—and he certainly was no more clear about what manner of woman she was than he had been earlier. Except, of course, that she was amusing.

There had been an apparent rift between Landford and Lady Genevieve, although Melville had not been able to discern the nature of it. They spent little time together, and she clearly was being courted by others. He had heard no formal announcement of their engagement, nor even any gossip about it.

He wondered if possibly Landford had already regretted his earlier actions and had broken the engagement. Watching the boy's face that night as he in turn watched Lady Genevieve on the dance floor had decided that question for him, though. The boy had not broken the engagement; he looked far too miserable. When Melville attempted to talk to him, however, Landford cut him short. Obviously, the young man had no interest in continuing the earlier, friendlier relationship they had enjoyed before the wager.

As he led Diana from the ballroom, he found himself wondering about her motive in asking to be escorted out for a breath of fresh air. He remembered very vividly the last time that they had done such a thing. In the days since then, they had had little enough opportunity for another such moment; Lady Rigsby had done her best to see to it that they were not left alone. In fact, he found himself looking over his shoulder at the moment they left, fully expecting to encounter Lady Rigsby or Landford—or at the least, Lady Lavinia.

To Diana's surprise, Melville escorted her to his carriage and lifted her in before she quite realized what they were doing.

"A short ride will give you the fresh air you need, ma'am," he remarked as he leaped in lightly beside her and the footman closed the door behind him. "And it will give us the privacy that we need in order to talk."

Diana found this a little unsettling. She had carefully rehearsed what she would say and do when they were alone once more, but she had planned to say it with people close by—certainly within shouting range. This was far too private, and she could already hear Lady Rigsby's biting commentary on her behavior. Still, she reminded herself, she must force Melville to commit himself to marriage if Trevor and Jenny were to be saved. She had seen their desperate expressions as Treffington led Jenny out onto the dance floor that night.

She forced herself to relax as he settled next to her—far too closely next to her, she thought indignantly. She slipped one arm around his neck and pulled his lips down to her own. "I had hoped that we would have some time alone," she whispered. "I have rehearsed this moment in my mind countless times."

And that had the undeniable ring of truth, she thought with satisfaction as she kissed him. To her dismay, he fairly lifted her off the seat as he crushed her against him, sending her carefully arranged curls tumbling over her shoulders.

"Let me go, sir!" she exclaimed angrily, trying to

believe that she had not responded and pushing him away as firmly as she could.

"Is this not what you had in mind, Lady Diana?" he inquired, straightening his cravat. "Or did you plan to ask me again if I had spoken with your uncle?"

"Naturally I was going to ask you about Uncle Robert," she replied mendaciously, trying to set her hair to rights. He had no need to know the truth.

"It would do no good, you know, even if I agreed to see him tomorrow morning," Melville said suddenly, watching her face in the lamplight.

"What do you mean?" she asked.

"He would not give me your hand, for he would investigate and discover my reputation. Why would he allow me to marry you and your fortune?"

Diana stared at him blankly for a moment. "But you would not need even to ask him if you really wished to marry me," she responded slowly. "We could elope."

"Ah, Gretna Greene," he said, understanding. "Then we would not need his permission."

"Of course not," she replied. "But I see that such a thing had not occurred to you."

"I am aware of your opinion of me, ma'am, but it would not be just my style to elope with a young heiress. There are those who might doubt the sincerity of my devotion to you."

"And what would that matter?" she demanded. "You have always done just as you pleased and never minded about shocking people. Why could you not do that now?"

What did she have in mind? he wondered briefly.

"Perhaps I am more practical than you imagine, Lady Diana," he responded, saying the first thing that came to his mind.

"What do you mean?"

"Why, if I elope with you, your uncle can keep you—and me—from your money until you are twenty-five. That is quite a long time to wait for payment, my girl."

Before she could catch herself, Diana had slapped his face sharply.

"Now that is what I would expect!" he said triumphantly, catching her wrist before she could strike again. Suddenly, however, her arm fell limply, for she had remembered Trevor's difficulty. She would swallow her pride.

"You could convince Uncle Robert," she said urgently. "You could tell him about the wager."

His eyebrows shot out of sight. "Why in heaven's name would I tell him such a thing as that?" he demanded. "No guardian in his right mind would allow a marriage after hearing that the man in question had won his ward's hand in a game of cards!"

"But he would see that you could ruin me if you chose to do so," Diana said desperately. "You could force him to allow the marriage in order to prevent the gossip you could cause."

"Blackmail?" he asked, suddenly amused. "You do think very highly of me, I see. That would indeed be a charming way to begin our married life."

Diana's face fell. "You won't do it, then?" she asked. She had played her hand badly, she thought bitterly. If she had used her head, she could have brought him successfully to heel instead of alienating him.

"Just why are you so desperate to marry me?" he asked curiously. "I am not unaware of my charms, of course, but this seems an unusually strong reaction to them. I had not thought myself so devastating."

They rode back to the ball in silence, Diana despairing because she had made a mull of things and Melville feeling certain that he was far too powerfully drawn to this girl, who obviously was trying to use him for purposes of her own. He would almost suspect her of marrying him for his money were it not for the fact he had checked upon Landford and his sister. They would indeed both have substantial fortunes.

Melville sighed as he glanced down at her unhappy face in the lamplight. He had almost told her that he would go to her uncle. If he were not careful, he would find himself married, a situation that he had promised himself firmly would never be his. It was high time to break the tie with the Ballingers.

As they returned to the ball, he decided that this was the moment. Turning his back upon Diana after returning her to a table where her aunt was seated, he made his way across the room to Lady Genevieve. To the astonishment of all concerned, he led that young lady onto the dance floor, bowing to Treffington, who had also been bearing down upon the young woman, as he did so.

"What is he doing?" asked Trevor belligerently as he seated himself beside his sister and stared at the dancers.

"He appears to be dancing," replied Diana. She did not add that Lady Genevieve appeared to be enjoying herself, happy no doubt to be saved from Treffington.

"Well, I can see that, Di!" snapped Trevor impatiently. "But why is he dancing with her? That's the thing! I don't believe he has ever done so before."

"Indeed?" she responded. She really did not wish to discuss the matter. She could see, even at this distance, that Melville was smiling down into his partner's eyes—and he had such hypnotic eyes that she did not see how Jenny could fail to fall prey to them.

"Did you quarrel with him, Di?" asked Trevor in an anguished voice. He could see precisely what she could, and he was no more happy about it.

Diana shook her head. "I don't believe I convinced him to marry me, though," she observed. "Or, if I did, he has a most peculiar way of showing it."

About that time Tom put in an appearance and, seeing their expressions, asked in alarm, "What's happened? Has someone died?"

"Not yet," replied Trevor grimly. "But it could happen soon enough."

"Oh, come, Trev," groaned his friend, "no duels, you must promise me. No duels."

"Duels seem to me to serve a very worthwhile purpose," argued Landford, still staring at the pair on the dance floor.

"Not if you're arrested or have to race off to the Continent in order to avoid it," observed Tom matter-of-factly. "Don't believe you'd care for that at all."

"Well, of course I wouldn't," responded Trevor. "I'm not a basket case, you know. I can still think."

"Glad to hear it," said Tom succinctly. "Too many that can't, don't you know?"

There was a pause in their conversation at that moment, and the conversation of a pair of ladies seated close to them suddenly became audible.

"Yes, that's Appelby's oldest girl," one of them said. "She's too pretty to still be unattached."

Another nodded. "But from the look on Melville's face, she won't be unattached for long."

A matron in black silk laughed heartily. "I should imagine that Appelby is counting his lucky stars just at this moment. He is very fortunate to have a man like Melville interested in his daughter. The man has a fortune, you know."

Trevor and Diana stared at one another for a moment, each taken aback, then Trevor rose as though to walk to the dance floor. "I'll take care of this," he said between his teeth.

Diana and Tom together grabbed his elbow and pulled him back down. "Not like that, you won't, Trev," Diana said in a low voice. "We'll take care of this another way."

This was getting completely out of hand, she thought to herself. Trevor and Jenny would be hurt, and she was quite certain not only that Melville had no desire to marry Jenny, but also that he *did* wish to marry *her*. The fact that he had reacted in such a way to their meeting earlier in the evening had convinced her that he felt a very real attraction for her, one that he was unaccustomed to and that he was trying to hide—even from himself.

"How?" demanded her brother. "What can you possibly do that you haven't already tried?"

"I will tell you when we are more private, Trev," she said in a low voice. And she smiled. She would kidnap Jack Melville. There were stories about kidnapped brides being taken to Gretna Greene where they could be legally married, even if they were un-**derage**. This time there would be a kidnapped groom.

Tom, noting her smile and hearing her comment, once more felt the commencement of a dull, low ache in the area he associated with his liver. Life, he thought indignantly, was fraught with far too many difficulties. Someone should have mentioned that to him earlier so that he could have been better prepared.

Sixteen

Tom's liver was once again far more accurate than he wished it to be. Before they left the ball that night, Diana whispered to him to call upon her early the next morning and not to mention it to Trevor. Since his early morning calls upon her had been associated with nothing but horrifying experiences that involved him in matters which he preferred to have no knowledge of, the ache sharpened during the course of his brief and sleepless night. When he appeared in Diana's drawing room the next morning, he was haggard and hollow-eyed.

"Tom!" she exclaimed in some concern. "Are you ill? Can I get you something?"

He shook his head as he sank into a nearby chair, feeling that it would require much to remove him from it again. "Nothing to worry about, Di. I'll be all right again in just a tick."

He sat and stared at her blearily for a few moments, trying to prepare himself for whatever it was that was to come. It would be, he felt certain, traumatizing, and he did not wish his liver to be again taken by surprise. As swiftly as possible he marshaled his thoughts, considering again each of the nightmarish possibilities that his sleepless night had presented to him. It was possible, of course, that Diana had changed her mind and now wished to marry him. Or perhaps they were going gambling again. Or Diana could have discovered some other hapless soul with a large income that she was going to force into marriage. Or perhaps he was now going to play the role of highwayman and be shot while trying to seize a shipment of gold. Satisfied that he had thought of all the frightful possibilities so that he could not be taken unawares again, he nodded.

"Go ahead, Di," he croaked. "Tell me what's on your mind."

"You can see that we must do something about Trevor's situation," she said, watching him with some concern. She had never seen Tom look quite so out of frame as he did this morning. He was a pitiable figure. She paused, wondering if she should tell him, and almost decided not to include him. Further thought, however, convinced her that she must have his help rather than Trevor's. Trev was too emotionally involved to be reliable. Of course, looking at Tom at the present moment did not inspire confidence either.

"I know, Tom, that I can trust you," she began bracingly.

He nodded again. Of course she could. Neither of them doubted that.

"And I know that I can count on you to help me in any way you possibly can," she continued slowly.

He nodded his head with rather less enthusiasm at this. She could, naturally, but he knew that he would pay a considerable price for that help. Still, he nodded.

Impulsively she kissed him again on the cheek. "You are such a dear friend," she said encouragingly. "I don't know what I should have done had it not been for you."

Tom sat up a little straighter. Of course Diana and Trevor could count upon him for whatever must be done, no matter how painful. "What is it, Di? What do you wish me to do?"

"We are going to kidnap Melville," she said simply.

The shock of her words struck his liver with the force of a tidal wave, but Tom manfully managed to stay upright in his chair. Alarmed by his pallor, Diana hurried to pour a glass of brandy.

Pressing it to his lips, she said in some concern, "Are you quite all right, Tom?"

"Perfectly," he replied, choking somewhat on the drink. "Don't know why I didn't think of it myself. Kidnap him! There's the ticket!"

He stared at her for a moment. How many years in prison did one serve for kidnapping? At least Melville was not a Peer of the Realm, he told himself. Things could be worse.

"What will we do with him once we've got him?" Tom inquired. "Hold him for ransom?"

Diana laughed. "Of course not, silly! We're going to Gretna Greene!"

Tom stared at her blankly. "Gretna Greene? Scotland, do you mean?"

"Yes, of course Scotland," she said impatiently. "We cannot marry here because Uncle Robert would never give his permission, but once in Scotland, we can be legally wed."

"And I take it that Melville doesn't favor the idea of a runaway marriage," observed Tom dryly, beginning to feel slightly more himself. After all, he thought, in for a penny, in for a pound. Why do the thing by half-measures?

Diana shrugged. "Oh, he wishes to marry me, Tom—he just isn't aware of that yet."

Tom felt a sudden throb of sympathy for Melville. "So he doesn't know that he wishes to be married?" he inquired. "And what will we do if he still feels that way once we're in Scotland?"

"Oh, he will come round soon enough," said Diana confidently. "I am certain that he cares for me."

"Of course he does," said Tom, but she noticed that he did not speak with certainty. There was a lengthy pause and then he cleared his throat. "How do you know that, Di?" he asked finally.

She colored. "I am not really comfortable discussing that with you, Tom," she admitted. "Will you trust me, please? You must believe me when I say that it is true—even though he doesn't know it."

Tom had thought the matter couldn't get any worse, but obviously it could. Now he was having some degree of fellow feeling for Melville. Nonetheless, he would stick with Diana and do as she wished, even though he could see no good coming of it. If Melville didn't know that he wished to be married, it didn't seem likely to Tom that he would undergo a change of heart after being kidnapped and dragged off to Scotland.

"Yes, I'm sure it's true," he heard himself saying. How could he abandon her now? He thought briefly and longingly of what his life might have been had he not taken up a life of crime, then put that behind him and straightened his shoulders.

"Just tell me what to do, Di," he said firmly. In for a penny, in for a pound, he reminded himself. He had helped her with everything else. And he was certain that if he didn't help her, she would still find a way to kidnap the man.

Vauxhall had never looked more like a fairyland, Tom thought to himself that night as he strolled down one of the lighted lanes, listening to the light-hearted lilt of a distant waltz. He felt as though he were walking in a dream—or perhaps a nightmare. Ever since early that morning, when he and Diana had gone over the details of the kidnapping, he had felt as though he were taking part in a play rather than a real-life event. He could scarcely take it seriously at all.

In the distance a party of revelers, Diana and Jack Melville among them, occupied a row of supper boxes. Tom was strolling along the lane with a bottle of brandy laced with laudanum—but not too much laudanum, he hoped. He would prefer not to be brought up before a magistrate on charges of murder. Kidnapping would be quite sufficient.

He patted the flask, assuring himself of its presence, and turned back to the party so that he could mingle with the merrymakers. Once there he would await the opportunity to pass it to Diana, who would then slip some of the concoction into Melville's glass.

The party was a merry one, although it was definitely not one that Lady Rigsby would have approved of. Diana was supposed to be at a far more sedate evening party in Mayfair, but she had sent a note telling Sally Rigsby that she was indisposed and would explain everything to her later. Tom shuddered. Later. He preferred not to think of it.

Among this party numbered some of the younger people that Diana and Tom knew—some of the wilder ones, Tom amended as he glanced around the group. Since many of the young ladies were there without permission, a number of them, like Diana, were in masks so that their identities were safely concealed. Melville was there because Diana had sent him a note, signed with Jenny's name, telling him that she would be in attendance and would be watching for him.

"How did you tell him he could recognize you?" Tom had asked her. "You might get away with the height—you're only an inch or two taller—but what will you do about the hair and eyes?"

"A domino," she replied simply. "I told him that I would be wearing a light blue one. And it's dark enough that he won't be able to distinguish the color of my eyes clearly."

As Tom looked around at the group, he was able to find her immediately since most of the dominoes were black. She was dancing with a tall man also attired in a black domino—Melville, no doubt. She had told him to pin a nosegay of daisies to the front of his cloak, and there it was. Di and her dratted daisies, he thought bitterly. He took the flask from his pocket and started to take a drink from it, but caught himself in time.

That would be the final blow, he thought grimly: taking some of his own potion and falling asleep out here, leaving Di to the tender mercies of Melville. A moment's reflection revised this thought, however. If left to the mercy of one or the other, on the whole he thought he would prefer Melville.

When the waltz had ended, the two of them slipped into a box and began to eat. As far as Tom could tell, there was very little conversation taking place—which was no doubt just as well because Diana was supposed to be Jenny. Melville had put his arm around her, and Diana had quickly moved away. He saw her turn his way and he knew she had seen him.

Within moments, Diana had pulled Melville back to the dance floor, and Tom dutifully drew close to the deserted box. Seating himself lightly on one of the benches, he took a slice of the wafer-thin ham and began to nibble, pulling his flask from his pocket as he did so. Quite casually, he lifted it to his lips, but did not swallow any of the brandy. Setting the flask on the table next to Melville's glass, he left it there for a minute while he appeared to be helping himself to the food, then filled Melville's glass from the flask.

"Done!" he thought to himself cheerfully as he closed the flask and replaced it in his pocket, returning to the shadows to watch the action. Soon enough they would be able to put Diana's plan into action.

Minutes later Melville and Diana again left the dance floor and entered the box, and this time Diana allowed Melville to embrace her. Then she turned to her own glass and drank deeply, pushing Melville's toward him. To Tom's satisfaction, the gentleman also drank deeply, and he watched anxiously to see if Diana would be able to get him on his feet before the laudanum began its work. If she could not, Melville would merely slump over in the box and they would never be able to remove him unobtrusively.

He should have known, however, that he could place his confidence in Diana. In moments the two of them were on their feet and starting down a darkened lane, one meant for lovers. Tom followed swiftly and was there to help her when Melville began to sway drunkenly and then collapsed. Together they propped him against a tree out of sight of the path.

"We must have rats in our upperworks to think of doing such a thing," Tom announced, wiping his forehead with his handkerchief. "Only think what would happen if someone had seen us."

"But no one did," said Diana confidently. "Nor will they. The carriage is not too far from here. We will be able to get him there without anyone taking notice of us, and then we're safely off to Scotland."

She paused a moment and looked at him closely. "You're quite all right, aren't you, Tom?" she asked. "Do you feel up to following us in your tilbury?" This was the plan that she had laid out to him earlier. She and Melville would go ahead, Tom following close on their heels should she need assistance.

He straightened his shoulders. "Naturally, Di," he assured her, trying not to think of the long journey that lay ahead of them—with a kidnapped man.

"Then what's troubling you, Tom?" she asked patiently. "I can see as sure as the world that something is on your mind."

"Well," he said desperately, deciding he must say it now before it was too late to turn back. "Are you certain that you should do such an outrageous thing, Di?" he asked. "Trevor and your uncle will never permit your marriage to stand, even if we manage to get you to Scotland."

"What could they do about it?" she asked simply. "Once it is done, they would ruin my reputation beyond repair if they tried to interfere."

Seeing by his stricken expression that she had made a home point, she added, "Now do help me get him into the carriage, Tom, and then go and get your tilbury and catch up to us as soon as you can."

Together they managed to wrestle Melville to the end of the dark lane and into a waiting carriage. As Tom helped her into it, she hugged him fiercely and his heart misgave him.

"Let me come with you now, Di!" he said urgently. "What if something goes amiss?"

Diana laughed almost gaily, relieved to have the worst of the kidnapping behind her. "Nonsense, Tom. How would it look if he awakened and saw the two of us there? He would very likely try to take out his anger upon you."

"And you think that he won't do the same to you?" Tom demanded, determined now to go with her.

"No, of course he will not," she insisted, pulling

the door sharply shut. "And you will be close behind should I need you, Tom."

Signaling to the driver, she then blew Tom a kiss. "I'll see you soon, Tom," she called as the coach started slowly down the lane.

Tom sighed. He had known that things would be the way she wanted them to be, regardless of his fears. He turned to hurry down the dark lane, eager to reach his tilbury and begin his own journey. He was concentrating so intently on his plans that he failed to notice that one of the shadows began to move. So it was that he was entirely unprepared for the blow that struck him sharply behind his left ear. Without a sound, he crumpled to the ground and lay still.

Seventeen

When Melville came to, he shook his head groggily and then lay quite still, a wave of dizziness washing over him. For a moment he could not make out his surroundings nor remember what had happened. In the darkness, lying on the dark ground, he at first thought that he was once more in Spain, that he had been injured and left for dead.

Another minute or two assured him that was not so. In the distance he heard music and the faint sounds of laughter, then the sky was suddenly awash with fireworks. With an effort, he managed to recall Vauxhall and the young lady with whom he had been dancing.

"And what the devil happened next?" he asked himself, sitting upright and shaking his head slowly, attempting to clear the fog that seemed to have settled over him. "I was dancing with Lady Genevieve and then—ah, and then we returned to the box."

With a sudden burst of clarity, he remembered drinking from the glass she had pushed toward him, and then she had whispered that she had long wished to see one of the more private lanes at Vauxhall. But what had happened next? Suddenly he straightened completely and managed to stagger to his feet. What had happened to Lady Genevieve?

Returning to their booth did little to help him. No blue domino appeared among the throng, and there was no one he could question, for he did not know whom she had come with and he had no desire to damage her reputation by inquiring among the other merrymakers. Determined now, and with his head rapidly clearing, he rode directly to Lord Appelby's home on Cavendish Square.

If the butler was startled by Mr. Melville's abrupt demand to see Lady Genevieve at such a late hour, he concealed it well. Minutes later that lady appeared, regarding her visitor with astonishment.

"Mr. Melville?" she said, her eyes wide. "I had thought Terence had misunderstood. Do you wish to see my father?"

Melville shook his head. "I have come, madam, to be certain that you are quite all right after our evening's adventure."

Lady Genevieve stared at him blankly. "What adventure would that be, sir?" she asked finally. "I have been home all evening with the headache."

Melville looked at her searchingly. Certainly this was not a young woman capable of duplicity. He had noted earlier that she tended to be very factual and brief in all of her dealings; that was one reason her note and her behavior this evening had so surprised him.

"Forgive me, ma'am," he said, bowing to her briefly and turning toward the door. "Clearly there has been some mistake. I had thought—well, what I thought is of no significance. I was mistaken."

Lady Genevieve was left standing in the drawing room, staring at the door that closed behind this most peculiar caller.

Melville stood on the pavement outside her home, breathing in the cool night air in an attempt to finish clearing his head. Finally, he decided that the one thing to do was to return to Vauxhall to see if he could discover anything about his experience there. It seemed unlikely, but he could think of no other course of action for the moment.

The crowd had thinned substantially by the time he reached there, but he finally managed to find the waiter who had served them: a tall, thin man who looked as though he wished Melville and all of the others could be packaged up neatly and dropped in the Thames. Melville laid down a £5 note to get his attention; he had no time or patience for ramblings.

"Was there anyone else in the booth with the young lady and me at any time?" he asked.

"That much in your cups, were you?" asked the waiter with a grin. "I wouldn't have known it. You seemed quite all right to me."

"You didn't answer my question," Melville pointed out, his tone growing more irritated.

The waiter hurriedly pocketed his money so that the gentleman wouldn't have the opportunity to change his mind. "Well, not someone exactly *with* you," he mused. "I saw a young man in the box while you and the lady were dancing. I took him to be a friend of yours, for he was eating and looked quite at home."

"Did he drink anything?" Melville demanded.

The waiter looked somewhat startled. He thought a moment, then nodded slowly. "He had a silver flask that he tilted back from time to time."

"And did you see him after we returned to the box?"

The waiter nodded once again. "I saw you and the young lady leave the box and start out toward Lovers' Lane." Here he winked at Melville but drew no response, so he resumed his tale, disappointed. "The other gentleman appeared to be following along after you. Was he the young woman's brother or her sweetheart?" he asked.

He saw Melville take another note from his pocket and he grew more expansive. "I thought he must be one or the other when I saw him tail you like that. The thing I couldn't figure out, though, was who the last one was."

"The last one?" asked Melville, staring at him. "Do you mean there was a second man following us?"

The waiter nodded, his hand extended expectantly, and Melville, seeing there was no way around it, handed him another note. "Another nob in a black domino—a tall, thin figure of a fellow. I almost decided to follow along myself to see what was going on."

"How do you know he was—as you say—a nob?"

"Easy enough. Aside from ordering me around like he was a lord, he wore a gold ring that would keep me for the rest of my life."

"What did it look like?" asked Melville.

The waiter's hand opened once more. "It weren't no trumpery piece, I could tell that. It was made like a snake circling his finger, with a ruby for an eye. Not a piece I'd fancy myself, but it would bring a pretty price."

Melville pressed another £5 note into the waiter's palm as he turned and strode down the path that the waiter had indicated.

"The swells!" muttered the waiter. "Think that they can do anything they please." Then he became more cheerful as he examined the money. "But three fivers! That'll do the trick anytime. He can know anything I know for the right price."

Melville hurried down the path, passing several groves of trees and a winding path that he knew led to a grotto. When he found the place where he had awakened, he stopped and examined it more closely than he had before. He had been lying at the edge of the gardens, next to a little-traveled carriage road. The moon cast some light on the situation, but not enough for him to note anything of interest—if indeed there was anything to be seen.

What had happened? he wondered. He had not been robbed; he still had his money and his chain and his watch. And who had the young woman been, if not Lady Genevieve? And who was the mysterious young man? And he was quite certain that he knew the second stranger?

Slowly he began to retrace his steps to the supper box. As he made his way along the path, he heard a thrashing about in the bushes of a nearby grove. He stopped for a moment, listening, then continued walking. Undoubtedly a pair of lovers, he thought.

Something dropped on the path before him, and he bent to pick it up. Upon returning to Vauxhall, he had put on his domino once, and the daisies he had worn at the lady's request had fallen from it As he looked at it, the light began to dawn. Lady Diana! Who else was daisy-mad and bold enough to send him such a note, then masquerade as Lady Genevieve?

Striding over to the grove, he pulled the bushe aside to see what was making the noise. Looking down, he smiled.

"Why, Lord Ralston," he drawled. "It looks a though Lady Diana has trussed you like a Christmas goose."

And that, thought Tom bitterly, was precisely wha he felt like—the Christmas goose. He rubbed hi wrists and ankles briskly, trying to get enough circu lation going so that he could use them again.

"But what are you doing here, Melville?" he de manded as soon as the gag was removed from hi mouth. "You're supposed to be—"

"I am supposed to be what?" inquired Melville dryly.

Tom paused, trying to rethink his situation. Hi head was pounding desperately and he wanted to do nothing that would give Diana away. But why the devil wasn't Melville in the carriage with her, head ing north to Scotland?

His mouth was still dry from the gag, and inad vertently he reached for the flask. He had almos touched it to his lips when he remembered the lau danum, and he hastily recapped it.

"And why, Lord Ralston, did you not take drink?" inquired Melville, who was watching him closely. "I know that you must be thirsty after being gagged for so long."

"I don't feel like brandy," returned Tom quickly. "I've got the devil of a headache, but I've got to keep my wits about me so that I can find—"

"Lady Diana?" said Melville, finishing the thought for him.

Tom stared at him. "So you know about it then?"

Melville leaned over and pulled Tom roughly to his feet when he didn't answer immediately. "What should I know about, Ralston?" he demanded. "Who hit you over the head and trussed you up like this?"

Tom shook his head in genuine bewilderment. "I've no idea," he said. "I would have thought it was you if I hadn't known—"

"Hadn't known what?" demanded Melville. "Why are you certain I'm not the one who did this?"

Tom was still reluctant to answer, for he would have to betray Diana to do so.

"Well, will you at least tell me this much, Ralston? You followed Lady Diana and me, but did you know that Treffington followed you?"

Tom blanched and his liver lurched. "Treffington?" he said weakly, sinking back to the ground and shaking his head to clear it. "Then we must go after her. He must have thrown you out of the carriage and gone with her himself."

"Gone where?" asked Melville, seizing him by his lapels and hauling him to his feet once more.

"To Gretna Greene," Tom muttered, conscious of his perfidy and wondering if he were doing the right thing.

Melville stared at him blankly. "Gretna Greene? She was eloping with me?"

"Kidnapping you, to be more precise," replied Tom, starting to lift the flask to his lips once more. Then, remembering the nature of its contents, he poured it out in disgust.

"Drugged, was it?" inquired Melville, and Tom nodded silently, watching the last drop drain from the flask.

He looked down at Ralston for a moment. "I don't know why she would kidnap me or why she thought I would marry her," he said thoughtfully, "but I do know that we must do something about Treffington. He *will* force her to marry him, make no mistake about it."

Tom laughed a little bitterly. "I'd like to see him make Di do anything she don't want to do," he replied.

"That would be easy enough," replied Melville grimly. "If she is in his power, there is no need for him to wait for marriage before taking her. Once she is ruined, what choice would she have?"

Tom looked up at him, stunned. He was accustomed to thinking of Diana as capable of finagling her way out of any difficult situation. Stumbling to his feet, he said urgently, "What are we waiting for, Melville? Let's get on our way."

Melville took his arm. "*I* will be on my way," he said firmly. "I can move much more rapidly alone than in company. Just describe the carriage to me."

Tom managed to do as much, and then the two of them parted company, Melville to ride north and Tom, his head splitting and his liver aching, to find

Trevor. He dreaded hearing his friend's reaction to the news. At the best of times Trevor was excitable; under duress such as this, Tom knew that he would be quite unhinged.

And so it proved. Finding Trevor at home, Tom imparted the news, although he had to explain it three or four times before Trevor could believe that he had heard it all correctly.

"I'll horsewhip him!" Trevor announced violently, leaping to his feet and striding about the room.

"We'll have to catch him first," Tom reminded him, and Trevor hurried to dress. As Tom gave orders for fresh horses to be saddled, Trevor wrote a note for a servant to carry to Jenny, explaining what had happened and why he would not be able to meet her the following morning. Together they rode north through the darkness, following grimly the path laid out by Melville and, they hoped, the one being followed by Treffington.

Diana, in the meantime, had found herself in a less than desirable situation. After Tom had bundled Melville into the carriage, she had waved to him and sunk back onto the seat opposite him, grateful to have the worst of the undertaking behind her. Suddenly she realized, however, that instead of gathering speed, the driver had come to a complete halt. Before she could call to him, the door opened and a man climbed into the carriage.

"What do you think you're doing?" she gasped. "Driver! Driver, get rid of this man!"

"He'll do you no good, Lady Diana," said the figure affably, placing his hands under Melville's arms and dragging him onto the floor. With a brisk shove, he pushed Melville out the door and, before closing it, called, "Drive on!" With a sigh, he sank to the seat opposite Diana and pulled off his domino.

"Lord Treffington!" she exclaimed. "What are you doing here?"

"Now that is precisely what I asked myself about you," he returned, studying her. "Since your brother and Melville have been interfering in my courtship of Lady Genevieve, it occurred to me that I should pursue my interests with you."

"That will do you no good," she announced. "You must know that I have no desire to marry you, sir."

"Oh yes," he replied. "You have made that abundantly clear. But I decided to watch you a little more closely to see if there were not some way that I could help you to change your mind."

"There is no such way," Diana returned briefly. "I believe that you know that."

"Ah," he sighed, "but you ignore your present situation, ma'am."

Seeing her expression in the lamplight, he smiled. Tom had been quite mistaken, she thought absently, Melville's smile was not the smile of a crocodile. This man, however, had precisely that manner of smile— the white, sharp-toothed smile of a predator.

"I see that you take my point," he continued when she did not speak. "I must admit that I was curious when I saw you leave tonight and come to such a place as Vauxhall. I had thought you more discreet, and I am pleased to see that I was wrong.

That will make our relationship so much more interesting."

He smiled at her again as she did not answer. "Do tell me, ma'am, just what you had intended to do with Melville. The driver—whom I have now paid very handsomely, by the way—tells me that he was hired to take you to Scotland. I would suspect a runaway marriage, except that poor Melville appeared somewhat indisposed."

When Diana still did not answer but instead stared out the window with the determined expression of one who is hearing nothing, he sighed. "I suppose I will have to wait to hear that little story," he said. "Perhaps it will be our conversation at our wedding breakfast."

That at least won him a response. "You take too much upon yourself, sir! There will be no wedding!" she snapped.

"I feel that is the least I could do, my dear," he said gently. "I do not wish to ruin a gently bred young woman."

"I am not ruined simply because we have spent some time together, sir. Some young women might be ninnyhammer enough to believe such a thing, but I do not. Spending time alone with a man, even at night and in a closed carriage such as this, does not constitute her ruin."

"Oh, but that is scarcely what I meant, Lady Diana," returned Treffington, smiling again. "I believe that we both know what would constitute your ruin, however."

Diana involuntarily drew her domino more closely

about her. "My brother would call you out, sir," she said stiffly. "You had best think twice about that."

"Oh, I think he would not wish to publicize the matter," said Treffington. He leaned back against the seat and closed his eyes. "If you will forgive me, my dear, I feel that I should recruit my strength—and you would be wise to do the same. The driver has orders to stop at a little inn I know. We should reach there in a few hours."

Diana stared at him in disbelief. He could not mean such a thing, surely. Then, thinking of what she had heard of him and staring at the serpent ring he wore with such pride, she was suddenly certain that he meant precisely what he said. If he had his way, the morning would indeed bring her ruin. And even if she married him later, a more dismal future she could scarcely have conjured for herself than life as Lady Treffington.

Eighteen

Robert Barton looked up from his desk, his bushy white eyebrows drawn close together at this unwelcome interruption. He made it a habit to rise at dawn and begin his work, even when away from home and living in temporary quarters as he was now.

"Well, what is it?" he barked. "What do you wish with me, young woman?"

"I am Lady Genevieve Linden, Lord Appelby's daughter," said his visitor in a quiet voice, ignoring his gruffness.

"Yes, I know that you are," he snapped. "My man told me as much when he announced you. My question was why you are here."

"I am here because of this," she replied, placing Trevor's note on the desk in front of him. She watched him read it, his face flushing an apoplectic shade of red.

"What does this mean?" he demanded, waving it at her.

"I believe it means precisely what it says. Trevor and Lord Ralston have ridden after Lady Diana and Mr. Melville." Trevor had not been able to bring himself to tell Jenny that Treffington had entered the scene. His note had simply left matters as they were originally: Diana and Melville were going to Gretna Greene.

"And he believes they have eloped?" the old man exploded, rising from his chair and coming around the desk to stand close to her.

Lady Genevieve nodded, holding her ground. "That appears to be the case, Mr. Barton."

"Very likely true—just what I might have expected from that headstrong, thoughtless girl!" he muttered, then turned sharply to his guest. "And why did you come to me with this, ma'am?" he demanded. "Why not go to their aunt with this information?"

"Because I cannot see what Lady Lavinia would be able to do, Mr. Barton, and I think that something must be done immediately. They have several hours' head start, but if you make haste, you may be able to catch them along the way."

"And why should I do such a thing?" he demanded. "Why should I put myself to so much trouble and expense over this nonsensical matter?"

"Because it is not nonsensical," replied Lady Genevieve reprovingly. "Lady Diana could be ruined if matters are not handled correctly, and Trevor is perfectly capable of calling out Mr. Melville when he catches them. This could bring utter ruin to both your charges, Mr. Barton, but you might be able to restore some sanity to the situation if you but arrive in time."

Mr. Barton began to regard her with a more kindly eye. "I must say, Lady Genevieve, you have shown more good sense in coming to me than both of my charges put together have ever shown over any matter."

"Perhaps that's because you haven't given them a fair opportunity to prove themselves, sir," she remarked gently.

"I'm afraid that I must differ with you there," he replied grimly, remembering the countless times that they had disappointed him and laughed at him for reproving them. "But I do begin to think that my nephew did the first sensible thing I have ever known him to do when he offered for you."

"Thank you, sir," she replied, her eyes modestly downcast as she colored prettily. She was exactly the style of female of which he strongly approved. His niece, he reflected, would do well to take a page from Lady Genevieve's book—and so he would tell her once he had managed to run her to earth.

"Well, I thank you very much, ma'am, for taking the time and trouble to apprise me of my niece's misfortune," he said, rising and ringing for his man. "When I have returned from my journey, I should like to come and have a word with you, if I have your permission."

"Of course you may, Mr. Barton," she replied. "And do take care of yourself, sir—and remember that Trevor is very excitable. Do what you can to keep him calm."

"Oh, I'll keep him calm all right," his uncle said grimly. "I daresay there will be no calmer man in all of England after I have dealt with him."

Lady Genevieve was forced to be satisfied with that, and she retired to her home to wait anxiously for word of the travelers.

* * *

Diana, in the meantime, had not slept as Lord Treffington apparently had. Instead, she had kept her eye steadily on him, not willing for him to have the slightest advantage over her. As he slept, she had slipped from her bag a dueling pistol, one of a pair belonging to Trevor. While her captor dozed, she carefully loaded the gun, trusting that some careless jolt of the carriage would not suddenly awaken him.

No such mishap befell her, however, and by the time that her captor had awakened and dawn had begun to streak the sky with gold, she had the gun securely in her right hand, carefully hidden beneath the silken folds of the domino that she still wore.

When Treffington opened his eyes, he surveyed her carefully before speaking—quite as though, she thought to herself indignantly, she were some bit of horseflesh that he was thinking of purchasing. She was careful not to let her anger show, however. It was preferable to allow him to think that she was frightened. He would be less on his guard.

"I do think, Lady Diana," he said when he finally spoke, "that I have made by far the better bargain in selecting you over Lady Genevieve."

Diana restrained herself from saying that she was not a commodity to be selected, and schooled her countenance to express an admirable mixture of fear and supplication.

Treffington eyed her approvingly. "I see that you understand your situation. That will make all of this so much simpler for us both, my dear. When we arrive shortly at Barnard's Inn, I shall say that you are Lady Treffington, and we will be shown to our chamber."

Diana wondered bitterly how many other hapless victims had visited the inn, but she did not allow herself to speak. Instead, she devoted her time to considering her situation. Should she wait until they were alone in the inn before shooting him? If the people there were in his pay, as they very well might be if he made a habit of such illicit visits, perhaps it would be wiser to shoot him while they were still in the carriage. Then she would have only the driver and footman with whom to contend.

After another minute or two, she determined upon the latter course of action. Since she wasn't certain how far they were from the inn, her move must be made fairly soon.

"Where shall we live, sir?" she asked suddenly, forcing her voice to quiver a little as she spoke. "In London or in the country?"

Treffington stared at her for a moment, startled by this irrelevant question. He had sized her up quite differently, thinking that she would show more resistance than this. It was, he thought in satisfaction, a tribute to his own power to dominate the situation that she was acting in such a submissive manner. Undoubtedly she had come to realize his strength.

"In London, by all means," he replied. "The country bores me. Besides," he added, a glint in his eye, "how can I flaunt my lovely new wife before the *ton* if we are buried in the country? I shall wish for everyone to be impressed by your beauty—and by

your devotion to me, of course. We shall go everywhere together, my dear."

Diana scarcely managed to repress a shudder at
such a thought. "That will be a very pleasant change
from being buried in the country as I have been,"
she managed to say, attempting to sound grateful.

"I must admit, my dear," he replied, "that I had
not thought to find you so amenable to our marriage."

"Perhaps, then, you see there is no need for a
stop at Barnard's Inn," she said. "We could ride
straight on to Scotland instead—and arrive there
that much earlier."

"Oh, so that's what you have on your mind?"
Treffington returned, amused. "No, I fear that the
stop at the inn is quite necessary. It is, you see, my
insurance. Something could go awry before we
reach Gretna Greene, but if we have made our stop,
then your brother would not, I am certain, be willing
to see you ruined."

It was clear to Diana that he was greatly enter-
tained by the whole situation, and he added pleasantly, "I assure you that the business at the inn will
be taken care of very quickly and with very little
pain to you."

"I fear that I have misled you, Lord Treffington,"
she replied, her voice once more firm. There was
little point in playing the helpless female now, she
thought. He had determined his own fate. She
would have felt reluctant to hurt him if he had
shown some sign of mercy, but now that he had
shown no regard for her well-being at all, she felt
no compunction.

"Indeed?" he inquired, amusement still evident in his tone. "In what way, my lady?"

"I have not the slightest intention either of marrying you or of stopping at Barnard's Inn with you."

"But you see, Lady Diana," he replied patiently, in the tone of one explaining matters to a two-year-old, "you have no choice in the matter."

"And that is where you are, sir, most definitely mistaken," she said, smiling as she slid the pistol out from beneath the folds of her domino.

Lord Treffington blanched as he stared into its muzzle. "Put that thing away before you hurt yourself!" he commanded sharply.

"I assure you, sir, that I will do no harm to myself. My brother taught me how to use it, you see." Here she smiled at him. "I fear, however, that I will most certainly, at this range, hurt you."

He made a quick lunge for her, but Diana was ready, having practiced with the pistol as an amusement during the previous summer when Trevor was home. The noise was deafening in the small enclosed space and the smell of powder filled the carriage as Treffington collapsed against the opposite seat, blood staining his jacket.

"What the devil's going on here?" demanded the driver, jerking open the door. He had ground to an immediate halt when he heard the gunshot.

"There has been an accident," replied Diana gently, indicating Treffington, who was now busily bleeding onto the seat.

Cursing her and all of her ancestors, the driver climbed in awkwardly and attempted to stanch the flow of blood with the kerchief he had pulled from around his neck.

"Aren't you going to get over here and help him?" he demanded.

Diana looked at him in amazement. "Indeed I am not," she replied. "I—"

Before she could finish her sentence, informing the driver that she had shot him and was certainly not about to help dress his wound, she was interrupted.

"She grows ill at the sight of blood, you see," interjected Melville blandly. "She has always been tender-hearted."

Diana looked up quickly, coloring as she did so. There stood her intended kidnapping victim in the open door of the carriage, smiling at her affably.

"I think, ma'am," he continued, "that in view of that I should remove you from this situation as quickly as possible, before you are taken sick."

"You'll do no such thing!" asserted the driver. Then, catching Melville's eye, he added in a more respectful tone, "Someone's got to pay the dibs, sir. This here gent promised me fifty quid for this trip, and he only give me five before she shot him."

Melville looked at the driver for a moment, his eyebrows raised. "I believe that perhaps I should take both of you before the nearest magistrate," he said. "Did you realize that you were assisting in a kidnapping?"

The footman, who had been standing nervously alongside the carriage, burst out, "I knowed he was a bad lot when I seen him, Bert! Didn't I tell you so?"

The driver glared at him, but his own ruddy color had receded somewhat at Melville's words. "We didn't know anything about a kidnapping," he replied stoutly. "And someone owes me forty-five quid and the price of cleaning up my rig." He pointed indignantly at the bloodstained cushions and carpet.

"Then my suggestion is that you bear your passenger to the closest inn and provide for his care. I am certain that once he is conscious, he will gratefully fulfill his obligation to you."

The driver, whose prior dealings with the quality had made him less optimistic about such an outcome, looked doubtful.

Melville, in the meantime, had helped Diana from the carriage and deftly placed the pistol in one of his saddlebags.

"Did you have any luggage, ma'am?" he asked.

Diana pointed silently to a small valise and he collected it swiftly. Placing her on his mount, he swung up easily behind her.

"Here now!" exclaimed the driver. "You can't be taking her away! Who's to help me with him?" And he pointed toward the recumbent Treffington with his free hand, the other one still pressed against the wound. "And who'll explain how he came by that hole in his shoulder?"

"I am certain that your footman will assist you ably," replied Melville. "And you may count this your lucky day since I am not bringing charges against you for kidnapping. As for him," he added, gesturing toward Treffington, "I am certain that when he has time to consider matters, he too will be grateful that he has avoided charges—and that his wound was in the shoulder rather than the heart."

And so saying, he started back down the road toward London.

"We can't travel like this!" protested Diana as soon as they were out of sight of the carriage. Melville had his arm firmly around her waist, holding her against him.

"Are you so uncomfortable?" he asked gently, his lips so close to her ear that his warm breath stirred the curls there.

"Well, of course I am!" she replied tartly, attempting to counteract the strong inclination she felt to relax against him and enjoy the slow rocking motion of the horse. "And at this rate we won't reach home for days!"

"I quite understand your hurry, ma'am," he said gravely. "No doubt your family will be searching for you."

Diana had been wondering if anyone would realize before later this morning that she was indeed gone. Until the maid came to awaken her, it was very likely that no one would be aware that she was missing. She had tried not to think what Treffington had done to Tom.

"I should doubt that they know yet I am gone," she admitted reluctantly. "But we must go back to Vauxhall and find poor Tom! I only hope that Treffington did him no serious injury."

"Are you referring to Lord Ralston?" he inquired, still guiding the horse along at a leisurely walk.

"Yes, of course I am!" she snapped impatiently. "Oh, do go faster, sir! We must get another horse or hire a carriage so that we can move more quickly!"

"Lord Ralston is quite all right," he said calmly. "And no doubt he has alerted your brother. I daresay we will meet them on our return trip."

"How do you know that Tom is all right?" she demanded, twisting so that she could see his face.

"I found him bound and gagged in the bushes not far from the road where I regained consciousness," Melville replied. "And I was flattered beyond the telling, ma'am, to discover that you find my company enjoyable enough to wish to kidnap me and spirit me over the border to marry me."

Diana stared at him, horrified, then turned quickly around so that he could not see her face. "Tom told you!" she exclaimed. "How could he do such a thing?"

"He really had no choice, I'm afraid," said Melville apologetically. "And he was most apprehensive about your welfare once he realized that you were in Treffington's clutches."

This time Diana could not repress the shudder that shook her, and she felt his arm tighten around her comfortingly. "That man is a reprehensible snake!" she said indignantly. "Or not a snake—a crocodile! Tom was wrong when he said that you had a crocodile smile. It's Treffington who does!"

She was suddenly aware of what she had said when she felt his shoulders shaking. "I am delighted to hear that you credit Treffington instead of me with that somewhat questionable attribute."

"This is Tom's fault," replied Diana bitterly. "If

he hadn't planted the thought in my mind, I wouldn't have said it."

"May I ask just when Lord Ralston reached the realization that I bear such a striking resemblance to a crocodile?" he asked, his voice grave although she could still feel his shoulders shaking. "Was it perhaps when I came to dinner at your home?"

"No," she said crossly. "And you needn't try to make a May-game of me, Mr. Melville. I know very well you're laughing at me."

"I assure you, madam, that I am deeply affronted that Lord Ralston regards me in such a light—and I am relieved to hear that you do not agree with him. And while I daresay your brother feels the same way that Ralston does, I hope that your aunt does not."

"You know that she does not! I told you once that Aunt Lavinia has a very susceptible heart—and you have indeed won it."

"You flatter me, ma'am," he returned, but he suddenly sounded abstracted and Diana once more twisted round to look at him.

"So that is it!" he said suddenly, after studying her face for a minute and then smiling. "You are more audacious than I had given you credit for, Lady Diana."

"What do you mean?" she asked uncomfortably, turning her back on him again.

"You know precisely what I mean, ma'am," he said briskly. "Or should I perhaps say 'sir,' Lord Landford?"

Since Diana could think of no suitable retort to

make to this sally, she remained silent, staring intently down the road and ignoring him.

By this time they had come within sight of a modest-looking inn at the side of the road, and Melville turned down a narrow lane that led to the stable in the rear.

"I believe that we will talk about this over breakfast, Lady Diana," he said. "If our luck is in, we will be able to acquire a vehicle of some sort—or at least a mount for you, since you appear to take exception to riding with me."

Diana, once more acutely conscious of his physical presence, stiffened and held herself awkwardly away from him.

So occupied were they with their own concerns that they did not notice two riders pass the inn, urging their mounts northward. Nor did Trevor or Tom pay the slightest bit of attention to the inconspicuous inn as they hurried toward Scotland.

Nineteen

Since there were no private rooms to be had, Melville and Diana had breakfast in the taproom of the inn, sharing it with a pair of carters who appeared more intent upon their tankards than upon inspecting the newcomers. When he excused himself to make arrangements for their return to London, Diana sat quietly, trying to decide what she should do about her predicament.

He had not again referred to what he obviously knew—that she had impersonated her brother. Whether that was because they were in a public place and their conversation easily overheard or because of his marked preoccupation, she had no idea. What she did know, however, was that Trevor still had no chance of marrying Jenny and that Melville had said nothing of wishing to marry her.

He had, of course, come to rescue her from Treffington, but that could be simply because he wished to keep his investment intact—not because he had any real interest in her. He had flirted with her, but then he flirted with many women, as Lady Rigsby had pointed out to her time and time again. "He can charm anything in a petticoat," she had said flatly, "and you may be certain that he means nothing by it."

Sighing, she went upstairs to the small chamber that Melville had requested of the landlord so that she could put herself to rights before continuing their journey to London. Looking out the window, she saw him in the courtyard below, speaking with the driver of what was apparently their carriage for the trip. As she opened her bag, she saw the dueling pistol—and smiled. There was certainly no need to give up her original idea. After all, she knew how to reload the pistol.

When Melville finally stepped inside the carriage, the footman shutting the door smartly after him, he had scarcely managed to seat himself before Diana directed his attention to the matter at hand. She once more had slipped the blue silk cloak over her gown and, once again, she had used it to conceal the pistol.

"Ah, so you do plan to shoot me," he observed mildly, leaning back against the seat. "I had wondered when I saw poor Treffington if that was what you had planned for me had I been kidnapped."

"I certainly did not!" she replied indignantly. "Now lean out and tell the driver to head north instead of south, Mr. Melville. We are going to Gretna Greene!"

To her surprise, he did exactly as she wished with no protest, then sat back once more and regarded her with interest. "I am amazed that you are so determined to marry me, ma'am. And even more amazed that you would do this for a brother who was willing to stake you in a game of cards."

"He did not do that, sir—as I am certain you know by now. I did that myself when I posed as Trevor."

"And why would he allow you to do such a thing, to make such a sacrifice?" he asked. "You cannot deny that he knows about the wager now."

"Of course he knows about it," she replied impatiently, "but he did not wish it. Only think of it fairly, Jack." She ignored his raised eyebrows at her use of his Christian name. "What choice did he have? He wished to call you out, but he could not, for then everyone would have known of my disgrace. Anything he could have done would have discredited me."

"As I'm certain you pointed out to him," he observed dryly.

"Of course," she responded. "I assured him that you had no intention of marrying me, no matter what your bet was."

"Why did you say that?" he demanded, startled by her very accurate observation.

She smiled. "Because I knew enough about you to know that you wanted no ties of any sort, but that it would amuse you to enact this little charade and see how uncomfortable you could make us."

Disturbed by her knowing assessment of him, he said, "Nevertheless, there could have been some very unpleasant moments for you if you had been wrong about me."

"I would do almost anything—as you see—to help Trevor," she replied simply.

"Then he is a fortunate man to have someone hold his happiness so dearly. Few of us are so blessed." He stared unseeingly out the window, thinking of his own mother who had been unwilling to make such a sacrifice either for husband or son.

They sat for a while in silence, but eventually he looked at her closely, his mind once more on the matter at hand.

"May I ask, Diana—I will be informal since we are apparently so soon to wed—just why you are so determined to marry me? After all, your brother has won his bride. He gave Appelby the money, did he not?"

Diana nodded. "He did—but Uncle Robert refused him permission to marry, so he has no money to support a wife until he is twenty-five."

Melville nodded. "I see. And so you planned to marry me in order to—" Here he paused and looked at her expectantly.

"In order to support them financially until Trevor comes of age," she finished reluctantly, keenly aware of how crass this sounded. "Lord Appelby would never have allowed them to marry without an income, you see—well, actually Trevor himself wouldn't have done it because he could not have supported Jenny. So you see, I really had no choice. I had to force you to marry me."

Melville once more inclined his head gravely. "And I expect that it is a great sacrifice on your part."

Recognizing the laughter in his voice, her lips curved into an answering smile. "Of course it is," she said demurely. "After all, you are quite an old man, you know—some ten years older than I am, I believe. I am sacrificing my youth to you."

He nodded again, almost absently. "Doubtless Treffington would have been the wiser choice, had you only considered matters carefully. He might have left you a widow in only a few years, but I must inform you that I have every intention of living to a very ripe old age indeed."

As he spoke, he pulled her closer to him in the most absentminded way possible, quite as though his arm had a life of its own and he was totally unaware of its movements.

"That is not very accommodating of you," she returned lightly, snuggling next to him, her head on his shoulder. "And I do wish that you had pointed out the wisdom of marrying Treffington before I shot him," she added a little crossly. "I fear that he would not care to marry me now."

"I believe that is very likely accurate. He has always been a trifle sensitive and this may very likely have turned him against you." He looked down at the pistol, which she still gripped firmly. "I would point out to you, ma'am, that I might feel the same repugnance should you shoot me."

She glanced down at the pistol, which she had forgotten for the moment. "I think, sir, that I should retain this until I am quite certain that we are to be married. I would not wish you to cry off at the last moment."

Melville took the pistol firmly from her hand and kissed her, pulling away from her a moment to look into her eyes, and she was suddenly aware that there were no barriers between them. The intimacy that had sprung up between them so unexpectedly on the first night they met had deepened until it promised to engulf them both. As he folded her once more in his arms and pressed his lips to hers, there was no more thought of the pistol. Diana felt quite as though her soul was being slowly drawn from her and she returned the kiss passionately, warmed to feel that his arms tightened as she responded.

"There is not the slightest chance of my crying off, my dear," he said softly, his lips wandering to the hollow of her neck.

"Treffington planned to force me before we reached Scotland so that he could be assured that I would marry him," she murmured into his ear as he scooped her into his lap.

"We will stop long enough so that I may have the pleasure of shooting him, too," he replied, holding her tightly.

"There's no need," she said, stroking his cheek gently. "Trevor and Tom will be catching up with him shortly if they left soon after you did. I believe that he will be very well taken care of."

"And so shall you, my dear," he assured her. "If I receive but a tenth of the devotion that you have shown your brother, I will be a happy man indeed."

"Are you quite certain of that?" she asked softly, gently tracing the outline of his lips with her finger. "Perhaps you shall regret the marriage immediately and wish me at Jericho." She paused a moment before continuing. "I fear that I am inclined to be a trifle headstrong."

Melville had a sudden vision of Tom's expression as he had admitted being party to the kidnapping Diana had planned, and once again she felt his chest shake with suppressed laughter.

Suspiciously she studied his eyes. "And just what do you find so amusing about that, sir?" she demanded.

"I was thinking of Ralston," he admitted, giving way to open laughter. "I daresay it will take months for him to recover from all of this—and I believe he might describe your stubbornness a little more strongly."

"Poor Tom," she chuckled. "I believe he wished to warn you away from all of this, but he was too faithful a friend to betray me." Weary from her adventure, her mind drifted for a few minutes, lulled by the rocking of the coach and by Melville's gentle stroking of her hair as he held her close.

A sudden thought snapped her awake, however, and she sat up abruptly and stared into his eyes. "Just why are you now willing to go to Gretna Greene and marry me, sir? Why this sudden change of heart?"

He smiled down into her eyes. "Do you recall, my dear, the first evenings when you gambled with me, masquerading as your brother?"

She nodded silently, stroking his cheek.

"And do you recall how close we felt to one another, how easily we appeared to understand the thoughts of the other?"

Again she nodded, cupping her hand against the nape of his neck and pulling him toward her.

"I thought you a most extraordinary young man," he continued finally, when he managed to emerge from the embrace, "and I was determined to continue our relationship—until you again switched identities and I could no longer find you. I could not imagine what had come over Landford."

"Poor Trev," she murmured comfortably into his lapel.

"I am afraid I was thinking more of myself," he replied. "I have always been lonely, but I had grown accustomed to it—until I met you. In an instant you had ducked under the guard that I had so carefully set about my heart and made me care for you." He paused for a moment and his eyes grew bleak. "I discovered that I love you—even though I know how dangerous it is to put your faith in another person."

Diana took his face in her hands and pulled his lips down to hers. "There is no need to feel lonely any longer, Jack," she said softly. "I do love you—and I will not be leaving you."

His arms tightened around her as their lips met and once again Diana had the astounding sensation of being a candle melting in the flame. She did manage to emerge from this state for just a moment, however, long enough to gasp, "Shall we play a hand of cards, Jack, to see who will rule the roost? If I win, I shall call the tune. If I lose, you will listen."

He smiled down at her for just a moment before responding. "I see that I shall have a wicked time of it," he said mournfully. "I can only hope that Landford and Ralston will stand by me."

And crushing her to him, he put an end to any further conversation.

Trevor, Tom, and Mr. Barton stared down at the figure on the bed, his face pale, his bandage blood-soaked.

"She tried to kill me," Treffington moaned. "Pointed the pistol at my heart and fired."

"If Di had pointed the pistol at your heart, you'd be dead just now," observed Trevor briefly. "And perhaps you'd care to explain why my sister found it necessary to aim a pistol at you at all."

Treffington moaned again in response.

"And Appelby would have married Jenny to this fellow?" said Trevor in disgust.

Robert Barton looked blankly at his nephew. "That sensible young woman was to marry this man?" he asked in disbelief.

Trevor nodded. "Can you believe a father would do this to his own flesh and blood?" he demanded. "And if it hadn't been for Di, it would have happened."

His uncle stared at him. "Diana prevented their marriage?" he asked blankly. "How?"

Trevor and Tom stared at each other, and Tom could feel a telltale ache in his midsection.

"Why not sit down, Uncle Robert?" Trevor responded in an even voice. "This may take a little time."

Back in London, Lady Lavinia, left alone to endure the agonies of waiting, paced the drawing room and hurried to the window at each sound of activity on the street below her.

Finally a message came—amazingly enough—from Trevor and Robert Barton. It read simply: *All is well. Di shot Treffington. Uncle Robert approves marriage to Jenny.*

As she sat there, rereading the contents of the note for the hundredth time, another message arrived. Ripping it open, Lady Lavinia read: *Gone to Gretna Greene. We will name our first girl Lavinia. All our love, Mr. and Mrs. Jack Melville.*

ABOUT THE AUTHOR

Mona Gedney lives with her family in Indiana. She is the author of ten Zebra Regency romances and is currently working on her eleventh, which will be published in September 2001. Mona loves to hear from readers and you may write to her c/o Zebra Books. Please include a self-addressed stamped envelope if you wish a response.

BOOK YOUR PLACE ON OUR WEBSITE AND MAKE THE READING CONNECTION!

We've created a customized website just for our very special readers, where you can get the inside scoop on everything that's going on with Zebra, Pinnacle and Kensington books.

When you come online, you'll have the exciting opportunity to:

- View covers of upcoming books
- Read sample chapters
- Learn about our future publishing schedule (listed by publication month *and author*)
- Find out when your favorite authors will be visiting a city near you
- Search for and order backlist books from our online catalog
- Check out author bios and background information
- Send e-mail to your favorite authors
- Meet the Kensington staff online
- Join us in weekly chats with authors, readers and other guests
- Get writing guidelines
- AND MUCH MORE!

**Visit our website at
http://www.kensingtonbooks.com**